MW00667036

THANKS IN ADVANCE FOR READING MY BOOK.
PLEASE TAKE A MOMENT TO PROVIDE A REVIEW ON MY "FIVE KNOCKS" AMAZON.COM, BARNES & NOBLE, AND GOODREAD BOOK PAGES. I APPRECIATE YOUR COMMENTS AND FEEDBACK.

SINCERELY,
DONNA

Five Knocks

A NOVEL

Donna Vincent Roa

FIVE KNOCKS

Editor and Story Advisor: Olivia C. Matte
Editorial: Christina Safford, Jessie Foss, Eva Sclawy

ISBN-10: 09907331-3-0
ISBN-13: 978-09907331-3-3

Dedication

Kira An Schiff
Gretchen Marie Roa
Alexander Theodore Roa
Guli "Lily" Du

Acknowledgements

I'm blessed to have a supportive and loving spouse who believes in me and is a partner in all of my adventures. Victor Roa knows me inside and out and understands my propensity to be full of ideas and energy. He is not afraid of my strength, ballsy attitude, and brilliance. He consistently encourages me to fulfill my dreams and passions, whatever they may be.

This project, originally conceived and written as a screenplay, drew my attention to a pressing issue of our day: China's one-child policy. To jumpstart the creative process, Victor bought me seven books on screenwriting for Christmas, listened to the dialogue and scenes that I developed, and willingly took part in a family move to Hollywood when my screenplay got optioned.

During my tenure in Hollywood, I met an early champion for this story, Tawnya Bhattacharya, owner of Script Anatomy in LA who deserves special mention. She taught the screenwriting class in LA at The Writer's Center where I developed the initial concept, logline, and framework for this story.

Tawnya provided me with several rounds of valuable and constructive feedback on the early versions of the screenplay that served as the basis for this book. She has a talent for drawing out compelling and exciting storylines and training writers to love the art of rewriting. She is a writer's writer.

In addition to being a gifted storyteller and on the who's who list of Hollywood writers, Tawnya has the supreme ability to understand the mechanics of screenwriting, knows the precision required to deliver cutting edge dialogue, and possesses the creative acumen needed for compelling and believable story lines. She has keen insights on the dynamics of storytelling and a first-string coach's wisdom to guide any writer to their next level. I'm honored to call her a friend and colleague.

During my trip to the 2008 Cannes Film Festival, I met Sabrina Pi Chee Chen-Louie, an industry executive and filmmaker now leading JBF Entertainment, a Hollywood firm that shares Asian themes, cultures, and stories with the world. She reviewed my short film that premiered at Cannes and provided feedback on my full-length screenplay. In her comments, she challenged me to refine the original story and position it as solid relationship story. This book represents the essence of her direction. I'm grateful for her frankness and insight.

I would also like to acknowledge my late parents, Margie Broussard Vincent and Ronald Gene Vincent, who taught me the value of hard work and of an active curiosity, gave me the permission to ask why and explore life's possibilities, instilled in me the determination to succeed despite all odds, encouraged me to look at life with a joyful spirit, and taught me to value the healing qualities of laughter.

To my sister, Karen Elizabeth Perron, who I admire for her exceptional skills and talents in the creative arts and determination to always deliver excellence and precision in everything she does.

To my sister, Julie Ann Matte, one of Louisiana's great educators and school administrators, who contributes an unwavering belief in my capacity to achieve great things.

To my brother, Gene Thomas Vincent, who I deem as one of the greatest storytellers of our generation. He has a sense of humor that could engage a room full of people for hours. Gene inspired my interest in writing fiction and gave me a two-page scene treatment that I used to write *Possession Point,* my first screenplay. The set of characters included Sya. When I received coverage from a Hollywood producer, he told me that Sya was so strong that she needed her own movie. She is the main character in this book.

Table of Contents

The Deal

It was a rich, white man's club for the who's who of Washington's elite. Politicians, IT billionaires, and old money patriarchs typically walked the hallways of the Baltimore Country Club. Today was different. On this sunny Wednesday, a Chinese man dressed in a drab, khaki, government-issued suit walked through the beautifully framed doors with his small entourage of bodyguards.

Chu Shang, a Chinese government official, was in the U.S. to prepare for Deng Xiaoping's visit. His official itinerary did not include this meeting. He headed directly toward the private, vast, mahogany-paneled ballroom and entered. The entourage shut the door behind him and stood guard outside of the room.

In the far left corner, he noticed movement but heard no sound.

Chu Shang knew the drill. He was used to the dark smoke-filled rooms where bad deals took place. He felt the hair on his neck rise.

He was there to meet Blanche O'Grady, a U.S. government employee who was all about business.

No niceties.

No small talk.

No warm, fuzzy exchanges.

He sat down at the expertly adorned, antique table inventorying the accouterments.

The gold and silver finely carved Maplewood pieces of the Anri Montsalvat medieval chess set were lined up with precision.

The room smelled of a half-smoked, expensive cigar. Chu Shang saw that one cigar was missing from the box of luxury Gurkhas.

A lighter with a gold-etched, Chinese dragon lay near the cigar box.

To his left sat a bottle of 50-year-old, single malt, Yamazaki bourbon and a Kagami Crystal Company hand-blown, hand-cut decanter.

Chu Shang looked across the table and remarked about the items.

"An Italian-made chess set. A Chinese dragon on the lighter. Good. Beautiful. But, Japanese bourbon and Japanese crystal?" Chu Shang said.

"You were always one to notice the details," O'Grady said. "I like that about you, Chu Shang. You know as well as I do, there are just some things we can't control. Anyway, China's not known for its bourbon, and I know how much you enjoy a good bourbon."

Chu Shang was familiar with Blanche O'Grady's broad shoulders, brusque style, and near-choreographed masculine mannerisms. Her stark black pantsuits and precision-cut short hair made you think you were talking to a man.

She confused the senses.

This wasn't the first time Chu Shang had interacted with the solidly confident woman he called "the government man-girl."

Blanche O'Grady was a woman of power and behind-the-scenes influence and connections in Washington.

A high-ranking State Department official in the Nixon administration, O'Grady was part of a secret delegation to China that helped set the stage for President Nixon's 1972 visit. She was one of Washington's power brokers.

As a follow-on requirement to that visit, she was tasked to secure China's support for the U.S.'s two-child global population strategy – outlined in the infamous National Security Study Memorandum 200 (NSSM200).

O'Grady arranged for this side meeting with Chu Shang to remedy a situation that posed a national security threat to the U.S. – China's overpopulation. She met Chu Shang during that secret mission to China and knew that he carried the same pragmatic, deal-making approach that made Deng Xiaoping popular.

Indeed, Chu Shang was a brilliant lead population scientist and personal friend of Deng Xiaoping, China's newly minted change-master and architect of a more forward-thinking China. He was in a position of power – the kind of insider power that Blanche O'Grady needed to operationalize her plan – a two-child policy. However, Deng was not aware of Chu Shang's interest in profiting from a backroom population control deal with the United States.

Now, O'Grady had her man. She was confident that she could convince Chu Shang, a pawn expressly identified by the U.S. Government, to create and stimulate leadership commitment for the NSSM200 two-child policy that had thus far gotten little traction under Mao.

O'Grady knew that Chu Shang would be highly instrumental in carrying out this barbaric plan to curb China's rapid population growth. He was in the perfect position to help her set the stage for widespread population control in China and stimulate a new way of thinking about its burgeoning population.

A boy from a family of six children, Chu Shang was aware that China's current and expected overpopulation posed a threat to the U.S. and had the potential to cause instability in the region.

He also knew that O'Grady saw him as a puppet that was in the right place at the right time.

Chu Shang came ready for the deal. A deal that could change his state of life. He wanted more than the below average life of a Chinese government official. He needed to break free of the shackles that the party line placed on his life.

O'Grady had the power to help him do just that.

As he stared at her from across the table, he noticed that her signature, siren red lipstick was slightly feathering at the edges like someone had penciled in the vertical lines on purpose.

He had kept her waiting far too long.

Not one to let others take advantage of the moment, O'Grady broke the silence.

"Chess?"

Chu Shang didn't want her to take control as she always did.

He opened the cigar box, handed her a cigar, and took one for himself.

He lit her cigar, paused, then lit his own.

"Do you consider this a game?" he asked.

O'Grady inhaled and drew air through her cigar.

"For old time's sake," she said.

She leaned forward and moved a pawn.

Chu Shang moved his pawn and took a puff on his cigar.

O'Grady moved another chess piece.

Chu Shang noticed that her cigar went out.

They both grabbed the lighter.

O'Grady squeezed Chu Shang's hand so hard that his forefinger touched his little finger.

She aggressively pulled the lighter away from him.

"Just make it your idea. Deng Xiaoping will see you as China's hero," she said.

Chu Shang didn't seem bothered by O'Grady's gravelly-sounding voice, aggressive behavior, and uninformed conclusions.

He knew what he wanted to accomplish.

O'Grady had already tried to convince him once before to orchestrate and implement a two-child policy in China.

This time, he came prepared with a counter offer. He planned to use the deal to open diplomatic relations with China and tee up China's most favored nation status and designation. He wanted to make sure he got a little something for his part in implementing this monumental transaction in and for China.

O'Grady moved another chess piece.

She drew another long puff on her cigar.

Not bothered by the deep breath she used to experience the cigar, Chu Shang leaned back in his chair and with his face toward the ceiling, blew a dense cloud of cigar smoke.

"O'Grady, you play me stupid. What's in it for China?"

O'Grady knew the dance.

"We'll open trade relations," she said.

Their cigar smoke further clouded the room.

Chu Shang leaned forward to study the board.

O'Grady was already offering him what he thought he would have to fight for.

He didn't answer.

He didn't want to show his cards too early.

He reached to move a chess piece.

O'Grady grabbed his arm, stopping the move.

"Chu Shang, what do you want?"

"You need me. Face it, O'Grady. China's overpopulation threatens U.S. national security. You seek stability in the region. Even at the expense of human rights. Don't make this a discussion about economics or access to resources."

O'Grady twisted Chu Shang's arm.

Chu Shang responded with a forced smile.

"What's in it for me, O'Grady?"

She released Chu Shang's arm.

"Two million dollars...for a two-child policy," she said.

Chu Shang completed the move and stared proudly at his chess piece. Without moving his face, he shifted his beady-eyed gaze to O'Grady.

"Check. I'll do you one better."

O'Grady sat motionless.

"Make it $20 million, and most favored nation status. With this, I'll create and enforce a one-child policy for all of China."

O'Grady was intrigued by the counter offer.

She placed her chess piece down getting out of check and blew a big puff of smoke that enveloped Chu Shang's head like a noose.

Chu Shang relished the silence between them, wondering if she would bite.

He waited.

"Chu Shang, you represent a mysterious land and a mysterious people. Your offer exceeds my government's expectations," she said.

As Chu Shang went in for the kill, he leaned into the light and looked up at O'Grady.

He saw that her black eyes were wet with excitement.

With an assured smile, he moved his chess piece on the board.

"Looks like checkmate. Deal."

Chu Shang and O'Grady stood up, did the perfunctory, courtesy half bow, and shook hands.

He exited first.

O'Grady lagged behind staring at the chessboard.

With her upper left lip curled up signifying that she just screwed Chu Shang, she watched him leave and snorted that odd breath that said, "I've won."

She grabbed the king off the chessboard, tossed it into the air, and slowly put it in her jacket pocket.

Never one to consider the ethical side of her actions, she needed an expensive souvenir to remind her of the deal. The deal of the century.

She took one last drag off the cigar, slammed it into the ashtray as she stood up, and bellowed an evil, victorious laugh.

In earshot, Chu Shang stood frozen outside the door.

His heart raced.

His breath quickened.

He felt an ache in his entire body.

He had just signed up for authoring and promoting the one-child policy in China.

He would lead the social experiment in 1979 that would rock the nation and destroy the lives of girls and their families.

School Anguish

In a middle school classroom of forty Baltimore inner-city kids, Sya knew she didn't fit in. She tried not to take up too much space, breathe too much air, or do anything to get noticed. That morning, Sya's mom had neatly braided her smooth and shiny black hair with eight zigzag cornrows feeding into two thick braids that fell a few inches above her waist. While Sya did identify with her hair, this wasn't her favorite hairstyle.

However, mornings were more relaxed when she didn't have to brush her tangled, long, black hair or fight with her mother about culturally relevant hairstyles.

She felt uncomfortable in the pink and white, hand-me-down gingham dress and the one-size-too-small, white patent leather shoes her mom bought from the Goodwill store for $4.29.

This was the second time she wore the outfit in the first week of school. She hoped no one would notice.

Never animated or one to speak out of turn, she stiffened when anyone initiated an interaction with her, notably Keith Sampson, the class bully who sat right behind her.

Sya never knew what he would do next. The anticipation kept her on edge. She worked hard to keep her gaze forward to avoid locking eyes with Keith.

On this day, his behavior puzzled her more than usual. He seemed different. Agitated.

He exhibited an uneasiness that she hadn't seen before.

She listened to Keith aggressively tap his scissors on his desk and sensed that something would happen. She drew her shoulders up in fear.

"Heya. Chinese pea. Peapod, girlie girl," he said.

She never understood why he called her Chinese pea.

She wondered if he meant Chinese pee. He was cruel like that.

"Whatcha have for dinner last night? Egg dropped lo mein?"

"That's not a real dish, Keith. You're mixing it up, Keith. You're mixing up the words. Egg drop. That's a soup. Lo mein is a noodle dish. We don't have a dish called egg dropped lo mein, Keith," she said sheepishly.

Sya believed saying his name would diffuse his intensity.

She bowed her head and continued to work on the pink fish she was drawing. Sya liked the color pink, and she liked aquarium fish. They both represented calmness and freedom.

She hoped and prayed that the interaction was over.

As she turned her wrist to work on the tiny fish scales, she knocked over a jar of black paint. It splattered all over her dress and white shoes.

She leaned forward to pick up the jar and hurriedly tried to wipe up the paint.

She noticed that her 22-carat gold necklace with a distinctive "flower in a cage" heart-shaped charm had fallen out of the bodice of her dress. She hurriedly pushed it back down. She didn't want anyone to see it. This unusual necklace was connected to and represented her past – a mysterious past that even she didn't understand.

She continued to paint.

Keith remained quiet.

Mrs. Castette, who was working at the front of the room writing math assignments on the chalkboard, didn't see Sya's interaction with Keith or notice the paint spill.

Another teacher knocked on the door and motioned Mrs. Castette to step outside. Before she left the room, she pointed her index finger upward. The students knew that meant to keep quiet.

Keith had other ideas. It was the perfect time for him to make his move.

Kimmy, who sat to Sya's right in the next row, sensed Keith was up to something and gave him that "I'll take you on" look.

This brash, boisterous, green-eyed tomboy with flaming red hair, wearing ripped jeans and a Baltimore Orioles t-shirt, was her own kind of troublemaker.

Keith hesitated.

Leaning toward Kimmy, Keith whispered, "You. Red. Bettuh tun aroun' now," he said as he tapped Sya on the shoulder.

"If you don't, I'm gonna blindfold dis one here wit some dental floss. Chinky eyes."

Eyes wide open and fearing what would happen next, Sya looked at Kimmy.

"Do you think I should give him my lunch money again?"

"I'd give him a knuckle sandwich with spicy mayo between my fingers, then smear it all over his face," Kimmy said.

Ever the conciliator, Sya reached into her pocket and pulled out her lunch money. In her haste, she dropped a quarter on the floor and looked to Keith for permission to pick up the coin. She froze for a moment, unsure of what to do next. Then, she extended her hand with the remaining coins.

"Here. Take um."

Keith got up from his desk, towered over Sya, and slammed her hand down as he grabbed the money and put it in his shirt pocket.

Breathing hard and fighting back tears, Sya faced forward and shrunk into her seat, wondering what Keith would do next.

The silence in the room was overbearing. All of the other children knew Keith's antics and didn't want to be his next target. They would quickly turn around to see what was going on, then face front so he couldn't lock eyes with them.

"Thank you, little Miss Ching Chong. Whatcha doin' in dis school anyways?"

With scissors in hand, he reached for one braid, yanked it and her flew head back in a whiplash fashion.

Sya nearly fell out of her chair.

"Yuh not black. Why ya gotta wear ya hair like dis?"

He cut off the braid.

Sya screamed.

Keith wasted no time.

He rapidly cut off the second braid.

"Yuh not American either. Go back to chinky land," Keith said.

He threw both braids at Sya. They hit her in the face and stung her already wet eyes.

"Stop!" she screamed.

Pandemonium ensued in the classroom.

Several more boys joined in the bullying and yelled in unison.

"Chinky land. Chinky land. Go back to chinky-chinky land."

Hearing the raucous noise from down the hallway, Mrs. Castette raced back to the room.

"Students. Stop! Now!"

Mrs. Castette reached up to the speaker and pushed the front office call button near the door.

"Mrs. Castette. Code blue. Code blue."

Before she reached Sya, Keith grabbed Sya's necklace and yanked it off of her neck.

Crying uncontrollably, she remained frozen at her desk.

Mrs. Castette raced to the back of the room to stop Keith from doing any further damage.

The screaming children raced to the front of the room, away from the action.

"Ti-juan, get Principal Ciccarello."

Kimmy couldn't stand what was happening. She took it upon herself to tackle Keith and pin him to the ground.

She sat on his chest to keep him from moving, and then slammed his head into the ground as she fought him for Sya's necklace.

Principal Ciccarello raced into the room and removed Keith from Kimmy's grip. She hauled him out and headed to the front office.

"Kimmy, get off the ground. I should send you to the office as well. Class, take your seats and remain seated."

Her tears pooled at the corners of her mouth. Familiar with their salty taste, she gently blew her lips to force them outward.

"My hair."

She held up her two long braids.

"Don't worry, sweetie. It's just hair – it'll grow back," Mrs. Castette consoled Sya.

"And what he said...he's right. My Mom is black, and my Dad is from a state where they hate blacks. And I'm from a country where they hate girls. I don't know my real parents. I don't fit in. He's right, Mrs. Castette. I don't belong. Anywhere."

As Sya said this, she dropped her two braids.

Immediately, Kimmy picked them up and held them as Sya cried.

Kimmy, a child of linguists who could read and speak Mandarin, noticed the Chinese character for the word daughter on the backside of the necklace.

She walked to Sya and handed her the braids and the necklace.

"I'll be your forever friend, Sya. Friends for life through thick and thin," Kimmy said.

Sya looked up at Kimmy and smiled through her tears. For once, she felt welcomed and accepted.

The Flight Home

Sam, a lanky, renaissance man with heavy-rimmed artistic glasses watched his baby girl Sya as she turned the pages of her bright blue adoption scrapbook. He pulled the loose threads in the couch and wrapped them around his fingers in a rhythmic fashion, careful not to make another hole. This couch graced his Nicholson Drive apartment when he attended graduate school at Louisiana State University in Baton Rouge.

While he loved his job teaching at Johns Hopkins University, his salary as a theatre professor didn't allow for extravagance, and a new sofa was exactly that. Madeline was used to the finer things in life, and while she never complained to Sam, he always wished he could offer more. He kept running in his head that mantra "money isn't everything," but some days, it didn't seem to work very well.

Today was one of those days.

The scrapbook on his lap reminded him of the struggle he had with Madeline when her parents offered to pay for Sya's adoption. Sam wanted a child more than Madeline, but he didn't want to be in debt to anyone.

Madeline, who had several miscarriages with Sam, insisted that the money was a gift, but he could never reconcile $40,000 as a gift. Sometimes, it made him feel like less than a man and as if he couldn't provide for his family.

Sam stared at his beautiful little girl as his mind raced back and forth about whether this was a gift or a debt. He knew that he had to let these thoughts go. This transaction did not define who he was. He had brought this up enough times with Madeline to know that the subject had the potential to escalate beyond ugly.

He treasured the depth of his love for Sya and the full heart feeling that he so immensely treasured.

He reached to touch the tip of her nose.

"Love you," he said.

She reached back and touched the tip of his nose.

"Love you, too!"

Madeline moved about the kitchen making excessive noise as she prepared her beloved Maryland crab soup. She enjoyed using the culinary skills she gained at L'Academie de Cuisine in Gaithersburg, MD, where she studied in lieu of college. Not one to excel in math and adapt well in a college environment, she opted for learning how to cook. Cooking fed her attention to detail and creativity. Food gave her a vehicle to show her love.

"Soup's a cooking, you two!"

Sya yelled back.

"Smells good. Blue crabs. They're my favorite."

Sam made pincher claws with his thumbs and forefingers and chased Sya around the room.

Her adoption scrapbook fell to the floor.

She jumped back on the sofa, and Sam held her waist as she picked up the scrapbook. Laughing, they plopped on the couch.

They locked eyes.

Sam's eyes watered. He felt what he called that happy raw nerve feeling as he relived Sya's adoption experience. This story would never grow old for him. It represented the start of something so good and was one of his life's defining moments.

"Tell me the story again, Daddy."

"Sya, when I held you for the first time, the world stopped. You were smiling and mumbling. It was like you were trying to talk to us. Trying to tell us something. Every other child we saw that day was crying like they were afraid. Not you. Not you, my sweet baby. It was like you were just waiting for us to take you in our arms. It was like you knew that we were yours. I'll never forget how I felt that day. This picture brings it all back for me. It was the most wonderful day of my life. I can't even describe all of the feelings and emotions that I experienced at that moment. We had been waiting for you so long."

"Daddy, go on."

"It seemed to take a lifetime for all of this to happen for us. You were the most beautiful child in the orphanage, Sya. Your face was like a cherub."

"A cherub? Is that a good thing, Daddy?"

"A baby angel. Your cheeks were flushed with a rosy color, and your lips were ruby red. Your hands were so delicate, and fingers so long. I was already thinking about piano lessons. Horseback riding lessons. Teaching you how to juggle. I could already see myself putting a glove on your hand so that I could play softball with you."

"How did you know I was right for you? For Mommy?"

Sya knew how to ask the tough questions.

"The moment we received your photo and information from the orphanage, I felt as if I could see so far into the future of all the things that we would do together. When we met you in person, I fell in love, Sya. You captured my emotions. You captured my heart beyond my wildest imagination. You helped me to understand what it meant to be a dad."

Sya picked up the tattered airline ticket.

Sam smiled as he recalled further details about the trip.

"What else do you remember?" she asked.

"So many sweet things."

"Tell me more, Daddy."

"Well, uh, you did cry all the way home. Mommy and I walked you up and down the aisles on the plane to try and soothe you."

"But I still cried?"

"You still cried. And cried. And cried. I'm sure that everyone on that long flight wanted us to leave."

"But it was a sweet cry, right?" Sya asked.

"You bet. You finally went to sleep about thirty minutes before we landed."

Sya smiled.

"Do you think they miss me?"

Always ready to chide Sya in the gentlest of ways, he said: "Who, the people on the plane? Well, I don't think that they ever want to see..."

"No, not the people on the plane. My birth parents."

Sam paused.

While he loved to tease Sya, he knew that he had to give a thoughtful response to this question.

"I'm sure they do, Sya. There's a special place in everyone's heart where they hold memories of the people they love. I'm sure you're in that special place in their heart."

With his right hand clinched, Sam placed Sya's hand on top of his heart and touched his left shoulder.

"It's right here. That special place."

"I want 'em to know I'm OK, Daddy. Can we ever find them?"

"You bet. One day, we'll go back to the Wulan Orphanage in Hong Kong. We'll find them. I'll be Sherlock, and you can be Watson. We'll gather every clue we can to find them, Sya."

"Thank you, Daddy!"

"And, I'll bring my magnifying glass," she said.

Sam mimicked holding a big pipe and adjusting an imaginary investigator hat on his head.

"Look out Hong Kong. Here we come," Sya said.

Sam wondered how and when he could make this happen but never doubted that he had to make it happen for Sya.

Happy Birthday Sya

Sam, Sya, and Madeline sat at the breakfast table eating eggs and waffles. Sam could hardly contain his excitement. Sya sensed his nervous energy and peered at him with wide eyes as if to say "what, already?" As she reached to grab his hand, her shirt sleeve touched the top of her waffle and smeared the butter and syrup up to her elbow and across the table. Madeline grimaced and reached for a rag.

"I admit it," Sam said. "I'm just not good at keeping surprises."

"Surprises? What surprises?"

Sya knew how to egg him on.

Someone knocked on the back door before Sam could answer.

Sya jumped up to open the door.

"Hey, Kimmy. Come in. Eggs and waffles! And real maple syrup from Vermont."

"A celebration or what? Real maple syrup! No, thanks. Had breakfast. Got done early. Wanted to come over and bother you."

Kimmy looked at Sam.

"Wait, did I hear something about surprises?" she asked.

Sam reached into his back pocket for an envelope and handed it to Sya.

"One more birthday gift for my dragonfly. Happy birthday! I can't believe you're 15. Your dad is officially an old man."

Hesitating, Sya studied the envelope.

"Is this what I think it is?"

She smiled at Madeline, who sat motionless and expressionless. Sam could hardly contain his excitement.

"Open it, Sya!"

"Dad, you didn't. You did? You did!"

She planted two kisses on Sam, two on Madeline, and two on Kimmy. She hugged Sam, and the two of them danced around the room, while Madeline leaned on the counter with her arms folded across her chest.

"Yea! Hong Kong! We're going to meet. Uh. OK, maybe meet. My birth parents."

Sam grabbed her as she pranced around the room.

"One for you, me, and Mommy. This will be our best trip ever. I even got us a free room at the Kowloon Shangri-La Hotel. Courtesy of Uncle Paul," Sam said.

Sya and Kimmy ran out of the kitchen both screaming with delight. Madeline placed her face close to Sam's and with steel eyes admonished him.

"You're setting her up for a big disappointment."

Neurotic Ambivalence

Sam knew he was in the doghouse with Madeline about the tickets he bought for the trip. Tonight, as he brushed his teeth, he sang "Ain't Misbehavin'" from *Porgy and Bess.* He always sang Broadway show tunes to avoid confrontations with Madeline.

He called it his "Broadway bubble." He felt protected when he sang.

For most of the song, Sam sang with the toothbrush in his mouth. Tonight, he took the toothbrush out of his mouth so he could belt out, "I'm saving my love for you." This was his favorite line in the song, and it reminded him of his love and commitment to his wife and daughter. He took pride in his devotion to his family. He peered around the door of the bathroom to ensure that Madeline heard him.

Madeline knew the routine and was irritated by his joyous mood. She had so many feelings she couldn't reconcile or didn't want to admit about Sam's plans.

Madeline was overwhelmed with the underlying fear she felt about Sya's journey to discover her birth parents. She felt a sense of neurotic ambivalence about the whole situation – like there was a war going on inside of her head. She wanted to participate, but she didn't want to participate.

Madeline loved her daughter, but she experienced a sense of loathing and insecurity about when she thought about Sya's search for her birth parents. The uncertainty drove her mad. She wondered how she would cope with being replaced or pushed aside if and when Sya found her parents.

More on this day than ever, Madeline felt like an outsider. Sam had initiated the first step in the journey. She felt hurt that she wasn't part of the decision, or more importantly, she didn't have a chance to veto it before he said something to Sya.

Dressed in her cotton Jockey nightgown, Madeline pulled down the bed, fluffed the pillows, adjusted the curtains, straightened the perfume on the dresser, picked up a hair tie off the floor, and turned the lampshade so that the seam faced the wall.

Madeline fixed things.

She looked around the room for what she could fix next. She always took action to bring perfection to her world or so she thought. She cherished her perceived strength as a fixer and fixed things when she needed to reconcile the turmoil she experienced in her relationship with Sam and with everyone else in her life. Madeline often wore herself out operating with the relentlessness of a woodpecker hammering a tree for an out of reach insect.

Sam continued to brush his teeth, hoping that the situation didn't escalate. He stepped out of line with Madeline when he planned the trip, purchased the tickets, and gave them to Sya without discussing with Madeline first. He reasoned with himself that if he hadn't done it this way, the outcome would have been different.

Sam was a show-off. He continued to hum loudly and vocalize in harmony with the buzz of his electric toothbrush. He slid left with a Michael Jackson move, then right as he extended his toothbrush up in the air. He leaned into the counter to spit and missed the sink.

"Really?" Madeline asked.

Madeline grabbed a rag and wiped it up.

"Oops! Sorry! Got a little excited. Ain't Misbehavin' does it for me every time. What a parrrr - tay we'll have in Hooong Kooong!" Sam said, stretching the vowel sounds with his distinctly Southern accent.

Sam reached for her hands and gently held them together.

"Really. Stop. Maddie. Live, why don't you? Sometimes perfection is not fun."

She jammed her face in front of his and spoke aggressively through her clenched teeth. "Why didn't you tell me about the tickets? I'm part of this relationship. This family. Are you now the designated decision maker? Did it feel good?"

Sam retreated.

Madeline continued the rant as she stormed out of the bathroom.

"Third wheel, yet again. Thanks for leaving me out."

Sam followed her.

"OK, game over, Madeline."

"You think it's a game?" Madeline asked.

"Wow, Maddie. It's an expression. Come on, I need for you to stop this."

Madeline plopped herself on the bed in defiance and stared at Sam with her lips pursed.

"OK. I get it. You don't like surprises. Get over it."

"Surprises, Sam. Is that what you call this? A surprise. Right."

"Maddie, what the hell is wrong with you? Tell me right now, what has this child wished for her entire life? Haven't you been paying attention? This trip is the very least that we can give to her. You know some adopted children wouldn't give a rat's ass about meeting their parents. Some kids never even ask about them. This desire – this one wish – has consumed her. I have never seen a kid so obsessed with trying to connect with her birth parents. Don't you get that? You wanna fix something. Fix your attitude."

Speaking under his breath so as not to wake Sya, he leaned toward Madeline.

"Let me ask you, why did we adopt Sya?"

"Because I can't have children."

"And? Anything else?

"My parents bought us one."

"Is that how you see this? Bought? Where is this coming from? I don't know you anymore. Maybe you can buy a child, but you can't buy your relationship with her. That takes effort."

Madeline turned away.

"I'm no good at it. This parenting thing. Did we force something that was just not meant to happen? Maybe my body didn't give me a baby because my mind can't respond to a baby in the right way. Barren in body and mind. That's me."

Sam couldn't bear to hear Maddie talk this way.

He softened and reached to hug her.

She pulled away from him.

"Maddie, give me a break. If I had told you about this, you would have given in and gotten the money from your parents. We can't continue to be dependent on them. We need to pave our own way in life. Our way. I don't want to be in debt to anyone for money. There is no reason big enough. Owing money is both a trap and a prison. I don't want to live life with that kind of burden. We already can't repay them for the $40,000 they gave us to adopt Sya."

Madeline snapped at him.

"My parents don't want that money back. You know that. They wanted a grandchild, too. Let it go, can't you?"

"For once. I'm proud that I can do this for Sya. I've been saving for this very purpose."

"Yea, behind my back. I thought we said no secrets.

"No, Maddie. You were the one that said no secrets. Hear me out. Ever since she said to me, 'Daddy, I want to let 'em know I'm OK.' It just broke my heart. When I heard that, I knew that this was a wish that I needed to help my baby fulfill. There's so much love inside of this little person who is our daughter. I can never..."

"What?"

Sam turned pensive.

"I can never bring myself to imagine what it means to have a force inside of you so strong and demanding that it colors your every waking moment, your every waking thought. Maddie, we'll never know that feeling. But, there is one thing I do know. We have to work to understand it and help her through this. I don't believe Sya will ever feel complete until she tracks down and finds her parents or experiences a search that takes her to a true dead end. She is mature enough to understand that this may not turn out the way she expects. But, she has to conduct and follow through with her search. We've got to be partners with her on this. I tell myself every day that I must dismiss my feelings, doubts, insecurities, or any other bullshit going through my head. I need to be ready for any joy or undesirable thing we may experience or learn in this process. Look, this is something she's gotta do. We need to be there for her no matter what we think or feel."

Madeline turned away, yet again.

Sam grabbed her by the shoulders and pulled her close.

"Please, Maddie," he said with tears in his eyes and hoarseness in his voice.

At that moment, Sam realized that he should have shared these thoughts before now.

"Maddie, Sya didn't choose to be abandoned or choose to be adopted. She had little to do with her fate. Thank God she was abandoned at an orphanage instead of down a street drain, some dumpster in an alley, or God forbid killed during the birthing process. Who knows why the hell her parents would do this, but it happened. It happened. She's here. With us. She's brought so much joy and life to us. You need to understand that this is one decision she owns. There is some kind of primal force inside of her eating away at who she is and fracturing her identity. I stand before you today not fully understanding the depths of what she is feeling. But, one thing that I do know, she needs to find her parents before this desire eats her alive. We need to help her. It's the very least we can do."

Madeline heard Sam say only one thing – her parents.

He said it twice.

Madeline corrected him.

"WE are her parents, Sam."

Sam reached to kiss her again. She pulled away and stared at the floor.

"Please let it go. Please, Madeline," Sam said.

Then, he walked away. She followed Sam into the bathroom and waited for him to say something else.

Nothing.

She put her hands on her hips.

Nothing.

She stared at him, but couldn't bring herself to say anything else. She realized he wasn't budging on this one.

Before she left the bathroom, she folded the washrag neatly, placed it on the counter, and smoothed it with both hands. She calmly stared at the rag for a moment, and then wildly slammed it on the floor.

In anger, she glared at Sam and stormed out.

"Hong Kong is for Sya!" he yelled.

Under his breath, he added: "Get over it, won't you?"

Madeline headed to Sya's room to see if the commotion had awakened her. She was sound asleep, clutching the envelope with the tickets to Hong Kong.

Madeline stood in the doorway and looked around the room to see what she could fix. In her neurotic frenzy, she straightened the room and arranged the three empty suitcases near the door.

The noise disturbed Sya, and she stirred.

Madeline froze.

She walked toward her bed and tried to remove the tickets from her hand. Seemingly still asleep, Sya gripped them tighter and pulled them to her chest.

Madeline leaned down and kissed Sya's cheek, then covered her with a blanket and walked out.

Sya's night-light illuminated her half open eyes as she watched her mother walk out of her room.

Lost Fish

The doorbell rang. Madeline peered out of the window and saw Kimmy. Madeline felt both relieved and annoyed by her energetic presence. She knew that Kimmy was good for Sya, but she could be so gregarious and downright annoying in a Betty Boop kind of way.

Before Madeline could fully open the door, Kimmy barged in like she owned the house.

"Kimmy's here! Let's get started, girrrlll. Where's my Sya?"

Madeline knew the drill.

"She's a teenager. Guess?"

They answered together and laughed: "Sleeping."

Kimmy raced up the staircase to Sya's room, knocked on the door as she barged in.

"Yo, Sya. Yo. Yo yo. You yo. Girl."

"You're listening to too many rappers. Uh, bad rap songs."

"Sya, Sya, Sya. Didn't you tell me to get here early?"

Sya yawned and rolled over.

"Did anyone ever tell you that you repeat yourself?"

"I'll show you repeat. This always works."

Kimmy took a deep breath, as she threw her arms up in the air. She jumped on the end of Sya's bed. Up and down. Up and down.

"One Mississippi, two Mississippi, three Mississippi, four Mississippi..."

"OK, already. I'm getting up. And you just said Mississippi four times. That's an upgrade."

Kimmy continued to jump.

On the sixth jump, the bed frame broke and crashed to the floor.

They fell over laughing.

The sound drew Madeline up the stairs and into Sya's room.

Madeline stood in the doorway with her arms crossed.

"Kimmy did it."

"No, you did it."

"OK, we both did it."

"Right. Get up the two of you."

Sya and Kimmy ran out of the room to the basement stairs.

"Race ya. Downstairs. I gotta get one more suitcase. I want to be the first one ready for our flight. Hong Kong, here we come."

Back in Sya's room, Madeline sat down on the broken bed and put her face in her hands as she stared at the floor. "Why?" She groaned to herself. "It's not until next month."

At that moment, Sya and Kimmy screeched so loud that they startled Madeline, yet again.

She raced down the stairway to the kitchen level and didn't see the girls.

She panicked and ran through the living room.

The girls were not there either.

Sya and Kimmy both screamed again.

She turned to the downstairs basement staircase.

Streams of high-pressure water spewed everywhere.

The two girls fought each other to scramble back up the staircase.

Kimmy was energized by the experience.

"Love the drama. I need to come over more often."

"Shut up crazy girl. This is serious," Sya said.

Sya screamed again.

"Dad! Dad! Come now. You need to see this. There's water everywhere."

She ran outside to get Sam.

"Dad! There's a pool in the basement," Sya yelled.

Sam raced down to the basement. He plunged into the water searching for the source of the leak. He motioned to Sya and Kimmy to stay upstairs.

Madeline paced up and down the stairs.

Sam waded through the basement trying to identify the source of the water stream and yelled to Madeline.

"It's the pressure regulator. It's blown," he said.

Sam struggled to turn off all the water valves as he looked around at the extensive damage. His office and computer equipment were hit the hardest. The papers that sat on his desk floated past him. The ping-pong table had water up to the net. CDs floated around him like lost fish.

Sam had to take action quickly before mold set in. His attempts at reaching a service company were unsuccessful. Frustrated by his flooded basement and not being able to reach anyone on a Sunday, he slammed the phone down on the table. Hearing the noise, Madeline came into the room to offer her kind of help.

"You know, we could go another time. We don't have to go now. There's so much that needs to be done when something like this happens. And you know, there's the problem with mold if we don't take early action. They say it's really hard to remove if you let it stay there too long. And, when you have mold, it can start to affect your breathing. You know the air quality of a house is affected if you have mold. When mold compromises your breathing, which can lead to a host of problems far greater than we would ever have the resources to handle. This whole situation is beyond overwhelming. Why would we need to burden ourselves with this circumstance and travel on top of it? You know how tiring travel can be…"

"Finished?" Sam interrupted Madeline as she took a breath fully ready to continue her rant. That didn't stop her.

"Then, there are all of these bird flu epidemics breaking out and the chance that we could get infected. And, what about food poisoning? You know not everyone has the same cleanliness standards. I feel overwhelmed just thinking about having to deal with so much. And, let's not forget the child abductions that happen. One brief moment not paying attention, and wham, Sya's gone. And, even if we..."

"Stop. Maddie, what do you expect me to say? This is about the trip, isn't it? This trip can't wait. For so many reasons."

"I won't go without you, Sam."

"Is that yet another excuse? The truth is, you don't want to go at all. Am I right?"

Madeline gulped her coffee.

"Maddie, put yourself in Sya's shoes."

Sya entered, and Kimmy stopped in the doorway.

"My shoes?" Sya asked.

Madeline stared out the window. Sya sat next to Madeline and waited for her to say something. She placed her hand on Madeline's chin and pulled her face around.

"I need to know who they are. I'm somebody's child. You can understand that, can't you?"

"Yes. You're my child."

Madeline stood up and stormed out of the kitchen. Kimmy followed and joined her on the front porch steps, letting the screened door slam behind her.

Sya started to straighten up the kitchen. She dropped a glass on the floor. It shattered.

Sam gives her that "it's going to be OK" look.

"Come here."

Sam hugged Sya as she sobbed.

Sam could overhear Madeline and Kimmy's conversation through the screen door. He didn't want Sya to hear it so he brought her outside on the back porch.

Madeline raised her voice louder.

"Please leave me alone, Kimmy."

"Mrs. P., I'm no psychic. Don't have high falutin' shrink qualifications for giving advice to troubled adults, and I certainly don't want to be a p-e-s-t, but…"

"Just say it, Kimmy. Get it out."

"Well, it's probably better for me to show you than tell you, Mrs. P."

Looking toward the kitchen to make sure that she avoided Sya, Kimmy pulled a reluctant Madeline into the house and up the stairs to Sya's room. She opened the large bottom desk drawer, pulled out a large three-inch, three-ring binder filled to capacity, and placed it on the desk. Some of the papers fell on the floor.

"She's gonna kill me for doing this. There's another box in the closet of the older articles and books."

Madeline slowly turned the pages of the binder.

She felt the room darken and close in on her.

Her shoulders tightened.

Her breathing quickened.

Sya had done her homework. A massive amount of homework. This notebook contained hundreds of articles and Internet research on what adoptees needed to do to find their birth parents.

Madeline knew Sya was far more ready than she was for this journey.

Sherlock

Weekends in May at Druid Hill Park brought out all kinds of people and all kinds of activities. On this day, Sam worked with Sya and Kimmy on the proper technique for juggling colored scarves and balls. Not far from the street, they were juggling on the side of the park where several young men were doing motorbike wheelies and drag racing with each other. The roar of the bikes sounded like an orchestra of tubas tuning at the beginning of a concert.

Sam had juggling down. You could say that he was an expert. He loved juggling like he loved Broadway tunes, especially with scarves.

Sam felt as if he was creating beauty when he was juggling scarves. They reminded him of birds and the beautiful patterns and flight formations that birds create.

"Start off with two. It's easier. Once you get the hang of it, you can go to three," he said.

Sya was determined to learn how to juggle and had already experienced that unbridled excitement you feel when you go three or more rotations with the three scarves. She felt a strong sense of accomplishment when she was juggling.

"And, didn't you say to cross your arms like this?"

Sam showed off his juggling expertise, and the scarves started flying. Sam knew how to put on a show.

"Like this."

Kimmy joined in on the fun, trying to mimic Sam with the scarves. She threw two up in the air, and when she threw the third one up, the other two fell to the ground. Her focus seemed to be on the activity in the park.

"I'm not so good at this," Kimmy said.

Sya squealed with excitement.

"Kimmy, look at me. I got this. Yea!"

She looked lovingly at her dad and smiled as if to say thank you. She appreciated the strong connection they had. She always had fun and was happy around him. She felt like she could be herself. He was so other-oriented and found so much joy in the simple things in life.

Sam watched her with pride but could sense Kimmy's frustration. He was good at noticing how people were feeling and when they might need a kind word or gesture. He was the quintessential Southern gentleman who was always inclusive and thoughtful.

"Let me know when you want to try the bean bags, these rings, or what about these balls? Some people do better when the items are a bit heavier."

Kimmy had given up on the scarves.

"Give me the balls. Maybe I'll do better with those."

Kimmy tried her hand with the balls. She accomplished three rounds of juggling and started screaming in delight. They all fell to the ground at her feet. She picked them up to try again. In her zealousness to quickly begin the rotation of the balls, she threw the red ball way out of control, and it landed near the street.

Sya watched Sam run to get the ball and noticed at the same time, the two motorbikes drag racing at high speed in his direction. From that moment on, she witnessed everything in slow motion. One of the men, driving with no hands, popped a wheelie, lost control of his bike, and collided with Sam. His bike landed on top of Sam and slammed him against the road.

As he fell backward, his voice eerily echoed through the park. "Sya!"

Sam's head hit the concrete, and the impact caused his head to bounce like the ball that he just run after. The biker slid across the road about 20 feet and landed face forward on the concrete.

Sam lay motionless on the ground.

Frantically screaming, Sya and Kimmy raced toward him.

Hysterical from what she has just witnessed, Sya landed on her knees and grabbed Sam's hands. "Dad! Dad! Say something. Please don't die."

With blood pooling in his eyes and coming out of his nose, Sam mustered up enough breath to sing to Sya, "I'm saving my love for you."

With that, he closed his eyes.

"No. No. No." Sya screamed.

A crowd quickly gathered, and someone yelled: "Call 911! Somebody, call 911!"

As the biker struggled to get up and walk toward Sam, the bike exploded and caught on fire.

Sya and Kimmy fell backward.

Two elderly men in the crowd dragged them away from the raging flames.

The flames engulfed Sam, as the crowd continued to back away from the extreme heat.

The rider, who had concrete burns on his face and arms, stumbled toward Sam.

Despite the blazing fire, he tried to pull Sam from under the bike.

Sya could see that Sam's plastic glasses had melted across his face, and the red juggling ball now looked like a marshmallow between Sam's singed fingers.

One family raced to the fire with their picnic blanket and threw it over Sam.

Sya, Kimmy, and the biker struggled to drag Sam away from the flames.

In a state of shock, Sya stared at Sam wishing that she could bring him back.

Sam was her world.

He lay still on the ground.

Lifeless.

Disfigured.

Gone.

Sya felt overwhelmed with the thoughts racing through her head. Sam was so much a part of her identity. She wanted to give him one last hug, but she didn't have the chance. Where would she hold him?

Sya fell on her knees beside Sam and wept uncontrollably.

"Daddy. Daddy. Daddy!" she cried.

Her screams reverberated through the park.

Kimmy grabbed Sya and held her close.

"Kimmy, I've lost my Sherlock."

Kimmy knew precisely what she meant.

Grey Boxes

During the week following Sam's death, Sya's bedroom became her prison. She didn't know if she could ever recover from losing her father. She was never good at processing a loss. The only thing she had ever lost before were birds, fish, and turtles. She carried with her the memory and trauma of those losses and often relived the details of her backyard funerals when she was feeling sad.

Birds were the worst. Sya was four when she lost Birdland, an expensive African grey Congo parrot that appeared one day on Sam's office desk at the university. An anonymous donor instructed Sam, who loved birds, to give it to Sya for her birthday.

Sya named the parrot Birdland. She had heard Sam sing Manhattan Transfer songs often and had remembered this one particular line – "it happened down in Birdland."

As she sat in her room, she kept playing Birdland's funeral in her head. Over and over again. It wasn't the same thing as Sam's death, she reasoned, but there was so much about that experience that felt similar. It gave her comfort in an odd way, because Sam was a big part of Birdland's story.

When Sya was in elementary school, Sam broke his foot after falling off of the front steps of their townhouse as they were racing out to get ice cream at Fells Point. He took six days off from work, and during that time, he spent each day doing *New York Times* crossword puzzles, reading books on creativity, and teaching Birdland to talk.

Sam taught Birdland to say three things: "Manhattan Transfer," "Still preaching the rhythm," and "Jazz, Mama, jazz." He deemed this as one of his proudest accomplishments and had fun retelling the story about Sya's excitement when she heard Birdland say his first words.

Losing Birdland was the first and only time that Sya felt that kind of grief that you would never forget – the sort of grief that causes your core to fray around the edges. She felt sad when a fish or turtle died, but not the full-blown adult kind of emotional pain she felt when Birdland died. Birdland greeted her every morning with "Jazz, Mama, jazz" when she came to the kitchen for breakfast.

On this particular day, Madeline was preparing breakfast and had heated up a large non-stick pan with oil to cook eggs. Sya and Sam were upstairs when the doorbell rang. Madeline raced to the door, opened it, and was greeted by two Mormons in their classic white shirts and black ties. She noticed that Elder Kinderson and Elder Paxton also wore the traditional Church of Jesus Christ of Latter-day Saints nametags.

After greeting her good morning and introducing themselves, they began asking her questions about what she believed. She tried to be courteous and say that she was spiritual, but didn't believe in organized religion.

They seemed so young to be walking alone, she thought.

She tried to change the subject and started talking to them about neighborhood safety. They didn't seem concerned about it.

While Madeline tried to end the 15-minute conversation, they continued to talk about their beliefs and ask her questions. Their conversation was interrupted by the kitchen fire alarm. The oil in the pan on the stove had created a small fire and a room full of toxic smoke that was billowing into the living room.

Madeline raced into the kitchen.

Elder Kinderson and Elder Paxton dropped all of their materials on her doorstep and followed her.

As Madeline reached for a glass and attempted to fill it with water, Elder Paxton yelled at Madeline not to put water on the fire under any circumstance. He reached for the stove knob and turned off the gas, then grabbed an empty pot on the stove and quickly placed it over the pan with the oil fire.

Within minutes the fire subsided, and Elder Paxton apologized to Madeline for screaming at her. He related his recent firefighting experience to diffuse the situation.

Sam and Sya heard the commotion and entered the kitchen to find Madeline, the two Mormon missionaries, and a dead Birdland. Sya's beloved bird lay motionless at the bottom of his cage. The dense, toxic smoke from the non-stick cookware had already killed Birdland. Madeline had heard about PFOAs (perfluorooctanoic acid) and how the fumes from nonstick cookware could kill birds, but never really thought about it again until that very moment.

Sya's curdling scream startled the missionaries and prompted Madeline to begin her solemn and repeated apologies for killing Sya's bird.

As Sam helped Madeline clean the kitchen, he watched Sya as she sat still at the table staring at the dead bird in the cage.

That was her pet.

He was gone.

"We should bury him," Sya said. "What should we use?"

"Aluminum foil. I can help you, Sya," Sam offered.

For the next twenty minutes, Sya worked to fashion a two-piece casket for the bird. The top part was a quarter of an inch larger than the bottom so that it would fit snugly over the bottom like a box with a cover. Sya squeezed the edges of the foil carefully to form the bird-sized casket.

No one spoke.

Sya held the bottom piece as Sam opened the cage. He retrieved the dead bird, which was almost the same grey color as the aluminum foil, and put it in the makeshift casket.

Before Sya put the cover over the bird, she reached inside and touched him. His beautiful grey feathers felt both soft on top of his stiff body as she stroked him one last time.

She and Sam walked outside to their backyard near an azalea tree, where they would bury the bird. She watched Sam dig the hole and bury her sweet bird.

Sam leaned on his shovel as he told her that Birdland had fulfilled his purpose here on earth and needed to go home. She didn't understand what Sam meant at the time, and she certainly didn't get it now that Sam was gone.

All she knew now was that Sam was dead, and he had not fulfilled his purpose yet. Why did he have to "go home"? He wasn't done with living, Sya thought. And, he needed and wanted to be with her on her journey to find her parents. Sam was her number one supporter.

Still in a state of shock from seeing her dad fall and burn to death, she didn't know whether to continue to think about the details of Birdland's passing, feel sorry for herself, or be mad at Kimmy for throwing the red ball that rolled into the street.

She ran the scene over and over again in her mind as if she had the power to change it. That movie included a freeze frame where the entire screen featured a close up of Sam's hand holding that red juggler's ball. For some reason, he didn't let it go, despite the fact that he had been hit by that motorcycle and was knocked to the ground. The only thing that made Sya feel better was to imagine that he was holding her heart. That thought made her feel better.

For Sya, Sam brought life to life. He was master at fun.

Sya always wanted to understand just what made Sam tick. He was so much a part of her identity and her move to emotional independence.

She often dreamed about how she could tap into his energy, deep love of music, and passion for play.

Sya thought Sam could conquer anything, even death. She never got the chance to tell Sam how much she admired him and appreciated the special bond she had with him. She still needed Sam to answer all of her "life questions" and experience the milestones in her life.

"Hello grief, hello bereavement," she said to herself. She couldn't help but remember that she had been abandoned twice – by her birth parents' decision to abandon her and now by Sam's death.

Each night, she would pull the covers up to her chin, tuck the bedspread under each shoulder as Sam would do, close her eyes and listen to his last words. She treasured the special goodnights that he shared with her. In this very moment, she recalled Sam saying to her, "we are never promised tomorrow" and "make the most of every day."

Sya wondered if Sam knew that he had a short time on earth.

She laid still in her bed thinking about every single detail of Sam's death and funeral. the funeral home parking lot overflowed with cars. The police directed traffic to the restaurant parking lot across the street, then escorted families into the funeral home.

She couldn't imagine that Sam had touched the lives of so many people, including his academic colleagues and many of the students that he had taught at Johns Hopkins University.

Sya had never been to a funeral before. She recalled that nearly everyone was wearing black, and that she felt very out of place in her bright pink "Sunday go-to-meeting" dress. No one told her she had to wear black.

Sya was afraid. She didn't want to talk to anyone. She felt like a stranger in this odd place. She didn't want the dead body look to be her last memory of Sam. But, she knew that she needed to bid him one last farewell.

Her eyes widened as she scanned the front of the room where Sam's body lay at rest in a simple, grey casket. It reminded her of Birdland's grey foil casket.

Sya counted the rows as she walked to the front of the room and looked side to side at all of the people in the room so as not to fix her gaze on Sam's casket. She also noticed that there were Kleenex boxes at each end of the rows and reached down to grab a few tissues.

Sya looked around the front of the room with amazement. Plants and huge flower arrangements surrounded Sam's casket and lined the walls. She had never seen so many plants and flowers in one place. Though they were quite beautiful, she fully didn't understand the custom.

Kimmy, who was at the funeral with her family, stood up, walked to Sya and hugged her.

"I can go with you to the casket," Kimmy said.

"I've never done this kind of thing," she said.

They walked together to the casket, and when Sya reached Sam, she fell over his body and cried uncontrollably.

Silence filled the room.

Sya didn't care.

She continued to cry.

Before she left the casket, she reached in and touched the tip of Sam's nose. It felt so cold.

"Love you, too," she said under her breath.

Sya closed her eyes. She never wanted to forget this moment. She only wished that she had told Sam how much she loved him many more times than she did.

The birds chirping outside her window startled her and awakened her from the trance of Sam's funeral. Still in the darkness of her bedroom, Sya tried to understand the depths of her sadness and figure out why she had let her life become so different. She had always been shy in general, but now it seemed that she was more inside of herself and not interested at all in connecting to others.

Sya felt as if she had lost her mojo and her reason for being.

Her relationship with Madeline had also disintegrated, and she felt no interest in doing anything or going anywhere.

Sya had quit communicating with Kimmy who tried, again and again, to connect to Sya and bring some joy to her life.

She reached for a tissue on her nightstand and wiped away her tears. As she did so, she looked down at her hands and saw that she had dirt underneath all of her fingernails. For one who was so meticulous about her grooming, she couldn't remember the last time she had taken a bath, washed her hair, or brushed her teeth.

If she breathed deeply, she could also smell herself.

Sya looked down again at her fingers. She couldn't believe that she had let herself become so disengaged with life after Sam's death. The shock, denial, anger, and depression that she felt following Sam's death replaced that strong unexplainable desire to connect with her birth parents, but she was nowhere near the acceptance phase of grief.

The birds chirped again, as if they were calling her to do something. With that insistent sound, Sya sat up in her bed, got up, put on a pair of jeans and a T-shirt, pulled her hair back, and walked inside her closet to search for an empty box.

She rummaged through the contents and pulled out a large, flattened packing box. She brought the box out, taped it together, and set it up next to the drawer where she kept all of her research about finding her birth parents. She began filling the box with the binders, notebooks, and hundreds of pages of articles that she had collected over the years.

At first, as she took each item out, she would pause for moment and read a headline or two before she placed the article in the box. About halfway through the exercise, she started aggressively throwing each item into the box as if she was taking out her anger on all of the papers that she had gathered about finding her birth parents.

By the time she finished, the box was so full that papers slid off of the pile. She threw a sweatshirt on top of it to hold the stack together and tucked the sleeves and sweatshirt hem inside the box. She picked it up and struggled down the stairs trying not to make too much noise.

As she was coming down the stairs, through the living room, and into the kitchen, a few of the papers dropped out of the box. She did not stop to pick them up.

She was on mission.

Nothing would stop her.

Nothing would get in her way.

Sya headed for the backyard. Sam kept a large barrel he used to burn things. She opened the back door and walked to the barrel with the intention of destroying everything that she had ever amassed about finding her birth parents.

In her mind, she believed that if she got rid of this evidence of the search for her parents that she would be able to deal more appropriately with Sam's passing. She didn't know how that worked, but she felt as if she replaced one overwhelming desire with another, she would feel happier or more at peace with herself.

She walked to the barrel with her box and set it down, then ran in the house to pick up Sam's lighter and lighter fluid. She knew how to start a fire, and she was going to burn all of the papers in her box.

Sya wondered if she had focused too much on finding her birth parents instead of valuing and appreciating the parents that she had right in front of her.

Now that Sam was gone, she couldn't change that. There was nothing she could do to bring him back.

Sya ceremoniously crumpled up eight pages and threw them in the barrel. She poured lighter fluid on the stack and threw the match inside the barrel. She jumped back when the flames rose higher.

"There is something to be gained from this ritual. Destroying all of these papers and what they represent will heal me," she reasoned with herself.

Sya was careful not to put in too many things into the fire to make it go out. She didn't know if her three-ring binders would burn, so she popped each one open and pulled out all of the pages. She threw in the articles and her handwritten notes at first in a page-by-page fashion, and then she started aggressively throwing them in as the fire burned more robustly.

As she watched the fire burn, she examined all of the thoughts racing through her head. Why was it such a big part of my day-to-day thinking? Why did I need to know? Why did I let this overshadow my relationships? Why couldn't I just have been happy with the two parents that I had in front of me? Did I offend my father when I kept pushing for this? Did it make him feel sad that I could hardly think of anything else? What was I thinking when it seemed that every time we talked, it was about me finding my birth parents? Would letting all of this go make me feel any better?

No matter how much she thought about it, she couldn't wrap her head around the deep-seated intensity and drive for finding her parents.

Sya fully believed that if she burned all of her research and notes that she would also destroy the unexplainable yearning. All she knew now was that she could not have both feelings going on at the same time. Her love for her father was beyond imagination, and now, he was gone.

When she put another stack of paper in the fire, and it was raging at its highest, she fell to the ground and started crying again.

She still felt disconnected and lonely.

She watched the top of the fire and the ashes floating upwards from the heat of the flame, then downwards as if to shower her.

Sya sat with her legs crossed and her head in her hands as she continued to sob. There was something about this fire burning that made her feel both sad and happy. She didn't understand why.

Oddly, she felt strengthened and empowered by this act of burning all what she had collected and hoarded over the years.

As she stood up and emptied the last box into the raging fire, she yelled out a primal scream that woke Madeline, who raced to Sya's room to see what had happened.

No Sya.

As she came down the stairs, she stepped on some of the articles that Sya had dropped. When she reached the stoop, she peered out of the window and saw the fire burning in Sam's barrel.

Madeline reached the kitchen and stood in the doorway as she watched the flames. She knew that this was a turning point for Sya and wondered if she should intervene.

At that moment, Sya collapsed again on the ground near the fire. Madeline couldn't hold back. She realized that she needed to be there for her daughter.

Crying uncontrollably, Sya struggled with Madeline as she pulled her away from the burning barrel. Madeline hugged Sya even harder even though she was squirming and trying to get away. Once she realized that Madeline was not going to let her go, for the first time in many years, Sya hugged her back. She needed her mother now more than ever.

Madeline looked at the box near the burning barrel and could see the articles about searching for your birth parents. She didn't know what this action meant, but instinctively knew that it was not the right time to ask Sya about it.

They walked toward the door and into the house. Neither of them said anything. There was nothing to say.

When they got inside of the house, Sya ran up to her bedroom and slammed the door behind her. She felt safe in her room and wanted to use her solitude to sort out all of the feelings that she was experiencing. She felt too vulnerable to talk to Madeline.

Sya didn't know what she wanted anymore.

She felt directionless.

Downstairs, Madeleine sat at the kitchen table looking out the window watching the fire burn. The symbolism of what she had just witnessed was eerily overwhelming. She understood on some level why Sya would do it, but she did not know her daughter well enough to fully grasp her innermost thoughts. She had purposefully distanced herself from Sya regarding the search for her birth parents.

Madeline was not one to admit her insecurities about how she felt about Sya's birth parent search. Her refusal to go to Hong Kong was less about meeting Sya's wishes than it was for her own hesitation in knowing the truth. She was afraid of the truth and the consequences of the truth. Her already strained relationship with Sya complicated the matter further. Madeline never supported Sya's desire to find her parents or the trip to Hong Kong, and Sya knew that.

Today, Madeline was pushed up against an emotional wall by what she had seen and experienced with her adopted Chinese daughter. She had so much to think about and work on as it related to their relationship. She knew that she must do a lot of soul-searching regarding their life without Sam.

While oftentimes she, Sam, and Sya would not get along or see eye-to-eye on everything, Madeleine loved Sam with all of her heart. She also felt very lost without him. Overcome by deep-seated grief, she now had to parse the dynamics of her relationship with Sya if she wanted to make it work with her.

While she didn't know what this action of Sya's meant, she knew that it represented a turning point in their relationship. Now that she was Sya's mother and father, figuratively speaking, it had to be a different relationship dynamic with Sya. She wondered if she was up for this challenge and responsibility.

As she turned away from the fire and looked at the front of the refrigerator, she could see the three tickets to Hong Kong under the watermelon magnet. She stared at them. They represented the possibility that the trip could still take place.

Sam had purchased insurance on the tickets, so she knew she had some time. She decided that she would not bring it up unless Sya did. And after today's fiasco in the backyard, she wondered if Sya would ever bring it up again.

Crickets and Hearses

Two days after Sam's funeral, Madeline woke up early. Not by choice. By crickets chirping in her bedroom. Usually, when the irritating washboard sound awakened her, she wanted to get up, find the cricket and kill it. But, today, she didn't want to kill anything.

While crickets typically annoyed her, especially when they were the alarm she didn't set, today, this cricket sound made her think of Sam and all of the things he loved. Like the sound of crickets. Sam's applied curiosity drove his interest in many different subjects and made him fascinating, she thought, but how could someone love crickets so much? She felt sad that she had never asked him.

In between the cricket sounds, Madeline heard what sounded like several automobiles drive up in front of the townhouse. Shortly after, she heard the loud, almost simultaneous closing of car doors.

Curious, she got out of her bed and looked out of the window. Four funeral hearses had parked in front of her house, and four men dressed in suits were walking up the sidewalk. Half awake, she put on a housecoat, patted down her hair with water, and brushed it in a ponytail, then proceeded downstairs. The doorbell rang as she reached and opened the door.

Three men and a teenager dressed in black suits greeted Madeline. She remembered Mr. Franks, the elderly gentleman from the funeral home who helped her choose Sam's casket.

"Good morning, Mrs. Porter."

"Wait, was there some problem with my husband's arrangements? Good morning. Mr. Franks, right?"

"Yes, ma'am. That's right. I'm Mr. Franks. Napoleon, Wayne, Charlie, and I are here with the delivery.

"Delivery? What delivery?" Madeline asked.

Mr. Franks looked at Charlie who suddenly realized that he had forgotten to call Madeline.

"Apologies we didn't call. Charlie, here, was supposed to give you a call to let you know that we would be coming over, and this was the only window when we could make the trip to come to your house."

Madeline was on the edge of delivering her trademark screech.

"You're kidding, right? Is this some joke?"

Charlie piped up in the calmest, "sorry I messed up, funeral home director-in-training voice" he could muster. His tone broke the ice with Madeline.

"We wanted to make sure that we brought them before they all died, Mrs. Porter."

At that utterance and Madeline's now quizzical expression, he realized that he was confusing the matter further.

"Wait, ma'am, I didn't mean to say it that way, and if I can..."

Madeline interrupted the now embarrassed Charlie.

"Look, it's seven a.m. on a misty Sunday morning. I'm in my robe talking to four men in black suits, and there are four black vehicles that typically carry dead bodies in front of my house. My husband died this week and was buried on Friday. You didn't come to bring him back to me, did you?"

The four men gave her a "we are gravely sorry for the interruption" look that stopped her tirade.

Madeline composed herself as she leaned forward to look outside her front door to see if any neighbors stood on their front steps watching and wondering the same thing. Four hearses in one place is usually not a good thing. Madeline felt overwhelmed by the sight.

"Sorry. OK, explain."

Mr. Franks began.

"Ma'am, if I may share a personal story. Your daughter was so distraught at your husband's funeral. Our Charlie here saw her crying in the family break room and reached out to her. He fixed her a cup of tea and sat down across the table from her as she stared at the peacock clock on the wall. She transfixed her gaze on that clock. It's an heirloom clock from my maternal grandmother inspired by the 18th-century peacock clock created by James Cox for Catherine the Great. Anyway. Too many details. For a brief while, she said nothing, but drank her tea and stared at the clock."

Charlie added to the story.

"I sat with her. After about five minutes of silence, she spoke. She said, 'I do like birds. Well, fish and birds. But, mostly birds. They seem free. They work hard to fly, but then they glide. They spread out their wings and work with the wind to glide. They enjoy it. The gliding. Well, I don't know that for sure. I just imagine it. If they could talk, I'm sure that's what they would say. I had a bird. It could talk. But it only said three things.' Then, she started crying uncontrollably. I sat there and waited. I knew that she had something else to say."

Charlie continued.

"Then your daughter said: 'My dad gave that bird to me. He died too. The bird.' During our conversation, she continued to speak of her losses and was telling me how she didn't know if she could go on. I asked her if there was anything that I could do for her. Just ask, I told her. We sat in silence for about five minutes. She drank her tea and gently cried that kind of deep-seated, emotional cry where, you know, the tears are flowing, and breathing is slow, but you're not making much noise. Your daughter looked at the peacock clock one more time as if it gave her an idea. I could see her left eyebrow move down about a quarter of an inch and her eye squint like this."

Charlie demonstrated.

Madeline was becoming impatient with the pace of his story.

"Go on," she said.

"She turned to me and leaned forward on the table and quietly asked, 'What's your name?' It's Charlie Samuels, Ms. Sya. 'There is one thing you can help me with,' she said. Anything, I said. She proceeded to tell me that she wanted us to bring all of the plants and flowers in the viewing room to your house. She pulled a pen out of her purse and wrote your address on a napkin. Now, Mrs. Porter, I have never gotten a request like this before. I don't know, Mr. Frank, have you?"

Mr. Frank shook his head no.

"We usually just throw the flowers away, and the family takes the plants most of the time. But, we've never gotten a request like this before. All of the plants and flowers. Sya wanted all of them. She didn't tell me what she was going to do with them at the time. But, I knew that if I, we, did this as odd as it seemed, it would bring her some bit of happiness. And, here we are!"

Charlie smiled so big that his gums protruded.

"So, you're telling me that these hearses in front of my house have all of the plants and flowers from my husband's funeral and you want to bring them in here...in here?"

"Yes, ma'am!" Charlie said with a twinkle in his eye. He felt proud that he had lived up to his word.

"Well, how can I say no to this? What kind of mother would I be? Let's get this started. No, how about you get this started. I will not go out in my robe to help you. Sorry. You bring them in. I'll tell you where to put them."

The men walked back to the hearses.

Charlie smiled broadly. He knew what this meant to Sya. And while he didn't know exactly how all of this would play out, he had upheld his promise to her.

One-by-one, the men marched back from their vehicles carrying the casket sprays, standing flower arrangements, potted flowers, and potted plants. Madeline had no idea how she would be able to accommodate everything they were bringing to her small row house. She decided that she would fill the kitchen at the back of the house first and have them place the arrangements against the wall, back to front.

As the house filled up, Madeline moved the arrangements around to maximize the space. There were a few that still had sympathy cards attached. She paused a moment to read each card, then was distracted by the arrival of the next arrangement. She should have removed all of these cards to help her remember who gave what and to write thank you notes but didn't have that on her mind during the funeral.

She would do it now, she thought. So many thoughtful people sent their sympathy wishes for her and Sya.

One arrangement had a beautiful grey ribbon with several silver foil star stickers attached – the small kind of stars that middle school teachers would put at the top of your paper if you made an A.

Madeline thought to herself how odd it seemed to see those two stars on each end of the grey ribbon. Tucked behind the ribbon curl was a small, unopened card that Madeline had not noticed before. She pulled it off of the arrangement, moved the five potted arrangements on the kitchen table, and sat down to read the note inside of the card.

"Dear Mrs. Porter, we've never had the pleasure of meeting, but I wanted to share with you our deepest condolences to you and your family. We also wanted to offer our sincerest love and appreciation to your husband, Sam. Oscar took Sam's theater class, and he treated Oscar like a son. Sam mentored him through a rough patch in his life. It was Oscar's idea to buy the parrot, but he didn't want Sam to know it was from him. It was his way of saying thank you without making a big deal about it. He knew that Sam loved birds and thought that this would be a nice gesture. I thought you would want to know. Sincerely, John St. Pierre."

Madeline had always wondered who gave Sam that expensive bird. Now, she knew. Oscar Ethan St. Pierre.

After Mr. Frank and his boys finished unloading the flowers and plants, Madeline saw them to the door and thanked them. As she watched the four hearses drive away, she could hear Sya stirring upstairs. She didn't know exactly how to handle the situation in front of her. Flowers from the funeral of her husband surrounded her.

Madeline would let Sya do all of the talking since she didn't know anything about what she planned to do with all of the flowers.

Sya came down the stairs and stopped halfway.

"Whoa. That's a lot of flowers."

Madeline watched as Sya surveyed the living room.

She ambled down the steps, and then peered over the stairwell to the kitchen.

Madeline said nothing.

"I wanted to hold on as long as I could," Sya said.

Madeline wanted to tell Sya that the flowers would eventually die too, but she didn't want to ruin the moment. She reached over to move a couple of potted plants off of the sofa and cleared a spot for Sya to sit down.

Sya headed to the couch.

She tripped on one of the legs of the flower arrangements and knocked it over.

Five others fell like a row of dominoes.

That broke the ice.

Sya and Madeline started laughing uncontrollably.

She reached to picked up one arrangement and knocked down two more.

They laughed even harder.

During this experience, they both realized that it had been a very long time since the two of them had laughed so hard or shared such an intense happy moment.

Sya picked up the last arrangement and sat next to Madeline on the couch.

"Sya, why did your Dad love crickets?"

"What?"

"Did he ever say anything to you about crickets?"

"Yea, he was fascinated with crickets. Well, crickets and dragonflies."

"Oh?"

Madeline waited.

"Crickets. Oh yea. Big time. Especially the crazy sounds that they make. He said that it's how they talk to each other. They made that sound with their wings rubbing together. Like this. He said they played their cricket violins mostly to call their lady. Oh, and he said that they use their ears in the front of their legs to hear, well, not really hear, but to feel sounds. There's an organ on their legs...uh, the word reminded me of a timpani drum, wait, I think he called it a tympanal organ or something like that. It vibrates in response to moving air molecules. Then some other thing translates that vibration into a nerve impulse that reaches the cricket's brain. Once when we were at Walmart in the brush and hair tie aisle, he pulled out two big pink combs from the rack. The ones with the biggest teeth. He looked up and down the aisles to see if anyone was watching. 'Coast clear,' he said. Then, he handed me one, and we started dragging our fingers across the teeth of the comb. Oh, my God, the sound was so loud. We both laughed and shouted crickets really loud. An elderly lady standing at the end of the aisle with her hands on her hips gave us a dirty look, so we threw the combs down and ran in the opposite direction. I'm sure that she must have thought we were cray cray."

Madeline listened.

"I miss him."

Madeline waited for more.

"I know, you're probably wondering about all of these flowers. You probably think I'm crazy, but I do have a plan. I asked Charlie at the funeral home what they did with all of these beautiful flowers. Dad was always into recycling. Charlie said they just throw them away. People see these flowers for just a few hours, and then the funeral home throws them away. I wanted to do something else with them. What if we take these flowers and make arrangements to give to other people? Can't we make someone else's day happy with these flowers? If Dad were here, he would be making the list of the things that we needed to make arrangements. These flowers may be attached to our sadness, but we can turn them into something beautiful for someone else. I figured that we could make about 60 or more medium-sized arrangements out of all this."

Sya turned to Madeline.

"Can you help me?"

She sensed Sya's pride and determination to do something good for Sam. This project, it seemed, represented a ceremonial act of closure and healing, perhaps for both of them. While Sya's request – "Can you help me?" – was about the flowers on the surface, she knew that that request meant something much deeper. This was about Sya's life and her deepest held wish that didn't go away with the burning of the materials in their backyard.

"Yes."

Madeline's answer represented a renewed commitment to Sya. She realized that her daughter knew her husband more than she did and that her husband knew her daughter more than she did. She didn't want to feel like an outsider anymore.

One of Sam's deepest wishes for Sya was for her to go to Hong Kong to find her parents. Madeline knew that now she must be a part of that and should step up and take over that mission for both of them. It was not what she wanted to do or felt comfortable doing, but she could see that if she didn't, she might lose her daughter to grief and despair.

Madeline realized that she must step up to the plate and work to give their lives meaning now that Sam was gone. She knew she had to do everything in her power to make Hong Kong happen.

Regret

The taxi arrived at the stunningly beautiful 56-story Island Shangri-La hotel property in Hong Kong that boasted of a 16-story landscape silk painting, a 140-year-old historically significant banyan tree on the hotel grounds, and more than 900 works of art on display in the hotel lobby and guest rooms.

Bellman Wu, who was in his late teens, opened the taxi door. Madeline exited. Sya and Kimmy followed.

"Welcome to the Hong Kong Shangri-La, ma'am. Let me get those for you," he said.

Sya giggled at the formality of the interaction and marveled at the cleanly pressed, ornate uniform that the bellman sported.

Kimmy witnessed Sya's amusement with the bellman and decided to show off her Chinese language skills. "Xie xie."

Madeline appreciated Kimmy's effort but was annoyed by her bravado.

"You gonna be our translator, right?"

"Sure, Mrs. Porter. I know just enough to get us in lots of trouble."

Bellman Wu eyed Sya.

"What's your name, ma'am?"

"Sya Cynee' Porter."

She laughed.

No one had ever called her ma'am.

Kimmy walked closer to Bellman Wu.

"My name is Kimmy Lancaster."

Bellman Wu, whose attention could not be broken by odd redheads who spoke perfect Mandarin, did not take his eyes off of Sya.

"Well, Ms. Sya, welcome to the Shangri-La. And, if there's anything I can do for you, don't hesitate to ask. Bellman Wu, at your service, ma'am."

Sya giggled again.

They followed Bellman Wu to the grandiose reception area.

Kimmy couldn't stand the attention he paid to Sya.

"Well, aren't WE popular, Ms. Sya, ma'am?

Madeline noticed as well.

"He's a cutie."

"Shhh. He can hear you," Sya interrupted.

"Well, he is, my dear child," Madeline said.

Looking upward and taking in the magnificent surroundings, Sya and Kimmy gaped at the two sparkling, gargantuan chandeliers hanging from the ceiling.

Sya turned around in a circle, taking it all in.

"This could fill an empty heart."

"I'm with you. I could get used to all this, including Bellman Wu. Do you think that he has a brother?" Kimmy asked.

Sya eyed the seven-foot flower arrangement and walked to it. She leaned into the arrangement and smelled and caresses the huge pink flower.

"Sya, don't touch that. Let's go. She dangled the key cards. We've got the room."

Kimmy, who always wanted to be one step ahead said, "Is the room overlooking the harbor? What floor is it? Sya and I can run up and down the stairs for exercise. I could probably do 20 floors and not get out of breath. How about you, Sya?"

"I'm in!"

"Go for it. I need sleep," Madeline said as the girls raced off.

Hong Kong

Madeline unlocked the door to the hotel room. Sya and Kimmy threw their bags on the bed and paraded around the room. Sya had never seen such opulence. Asian silks hung above the European antique bed, and a Chinese tea set and cherry Chinese cabinets accented the room.

Sya stood at the large bedroom window and stared at the beautiful and picturesque Victoria Harbor. Her eyes watered at a beauty she had never seen before. In some strange way, Hong Kong felt like home to her.

"Wow. Wow! Just look at this place," Sya said.

"OMG. Thanks, Mrs. P. for including me in this trip. It's gonna be awesome."

Madeline didn't share the girls' excitement. She turned away from the window and unpacked her suitcases.

Sya and Kimmy continued to explore the room, opening the mini-refrigerator, the closet doors, and the bathroom.

Sya ran into the room and started frantically digging through her suitcase, as Madeline neatly filled the hotel drawers with her clothes.

"What are you doing?" Madeline asked.

Sya grabbed a brush and barrette and proceeded to fix her hair.

"We just got here. Where are you going?" she probed.

"Downstairs to get a Coke. Come on, Kimmy."

"I'm in."

"Why can't you just get room service?" Madeline asked.

"For a Coke?"

Madeline shook her head.

"Or get one from that thing."

Madeline pointed to the minibar refrigerator.

"Oh, I get it. It's Bellman Wu," Madeline said.

Sya and Kimmy giggled and replied in unison: "Busted."

Madeline sat on the bed and removed her shoes.

"Come here, both of you."

She gave them a hug.

"What was that for?" Sya asked.

Madeline didn't answer. She needed that hug more than Sya or Kimmy did.

"OK, 15 minutes. That's it. Back here in 15."

Sya and Kimmy exited, shutting the door behind them.

As they walked to the elevator, Sya jumped up and clicked her heels together.

"I can't believe it. We are finally in Hong Kong."

Kimmy, who always offered undying support to Sya, shared words of encouragement. "We're gonna find them. You'll see. Hey, let's run down the stairs."

The co-conspirators skipped hand in hand down the well-dressed hallway to the stairwell.

In the room, Madeline looked around to see what she could fix. She moved the chair away from the bed. She straightened the bed covers and the things on the dresser. She placed the TV remote on the nightstand, aligned the glasses near the water bucket, and put the hotel postcards, in-room dining menu, and Hong Kong city tourist guides neatly inside the desk.

She slowly walked to the window.

She adjusted the curtain tiebacks.

Overcome with emotion, she stood in front of the large window gazing at the Victoria harbor. She placed her forehead against the glass and cried.

Don't Flip the Fish

Sya, Kimmy, and Madeline walked down the streets of Hong Kong, which were abuzz with activity. Girl children selling flowers swarmed around Madeline and Sya. Sya focused her attention on one of the street girls. She smiled back. That's what the child did to garner sympathy and get sales. It worked. Sya took money out of her pocket and bought all of her flowers.

The little girl hurriedly tucked the money in her pocket, bowed to Sya, and then walked away.

Kimmy grabbed Sya and Madeline's hands and pulled them toward a street vendor.

"Let's have some fun!"

"Really, Kimmy? Slow down."

The sound of street vendors hawking their cuisine drowned out their conversation.

Kimmy walked past Sya directly to a vendor who was taking porcelain bowls out of a small oven.

"Sya, it's put chai ko, kinda like a cake made with pudding. I like the ones made with brown sugar. Gotta dig that smell."

Madeline twitched her nose at the bouquet of distinctive, iconic, and odd smells.

"Yea, which one?"

Sya eyed another delicacy.

"Can we eat on the street? That vendor to the right offers stinky tofu."

Madeline walked closer to the stall.

"Well, that's appealing. Smells like rotting garbage stuffed in a pair of old socks."

Kimmy sensed Madeline's frustration.

"Well, Mrs. P., how about Cantonese? In a restaurant."

"Do I have a choice?"

Sya grew impatient with both of them.

"Whatever."

"Sya, I hate it when you say that. Can we just sit down somewhere and get away from all this commotion?"

"Really. It's Hong Kong. What did you expect?

"Well, we have to go through all these papers. Look, what about that place? Red sign, gold letters. On the right.

Sya pointed to a restaurant across the street.

"Or that one?"

Madeline winced.

"Just hope it doesn't say fried dog."

"I'll protect you, Mrs. P. Don't you let anything worry your pretty little head."

Sya walked to the restaurant.

"Surely, they have other stuff."

"OK, Kimmy. Be straight with me. Does it say fried dog? That one. Does it?"

"Kimster, gotta go pee."

While Madeline and Kimmy looked up at the signs, Sya pierced the crowd and entered another restaurant.

When Madeline realized she had lost sight of Sya, she panicked. She turned left. Right. Cars zoomed by. More people. More sounds.

Madeline yelled for Sya.

People stared.

"Sya! Sya! Kimmy, help me to find her."

"Hold off, Mrs. P. She can't be too far."

Madeline and Kimmy crossed the street, looking everywhere for Sya.

Madeline raced back across the other side of the street with Kimmy, and both peered through the door. They found Sya waiting in line for the restroom.

"Young lady, where were you?"

Madeline glared at Sya.

"Sorry."

Madeline smoothed back her tousled hair and wiped the mascara tracks off of her face. She had that 'I've lost my child' grimace and had already started crying.

"Sorry. I just had to go to the restroom. I thought you guys were behind me."

Madeline grabbed Sya by the arm and squeezed it tight.

"Sya, don't ever do that again."

"I'm sorry. I thought that you guys were behind me. I won't do it again."

The restaurateur interrupted the conversation.

"Good afternoon, radies."

Sya was relieved he broke the tension. She gently smiled at the way he said ladies, then said hello.

Kimmy answered him in Chinese.

"Good afternoon, sir. Jasmine tea, please."

"Redhead girl speaka Chinese. Too cute. OK. You hih for Cantonese foo or Sichuan foo? Dim sum? All vely spicy. You rike spicy foo?"

Kimmy chimed in. This time she responded in English.

"I'm with ya on all that."

Sya marveled at the way he said food without the "d." "It was kinda cute," she thought.

He seated the three of them.

Within minutes, a second waiter brought the tea that Kimmy had ordered. He poured the tea as he watched Sya and Kimmy examine the surroundings.

Madeline discreetly wiped the mascara off of her face and reapplied her lipstick.

Sya could see that she was agitated by what had just happened.

"Sorry. I didn't mean to upset you. I promise to be more careful."

The waiter returned to the table.

"Can we try the steamed fish appetizer?" Sya asked.

The waiter didn't respond.

"This one doesn't understand English," Kimmy said. "Let me ask him in Chinese. Steamed fish, please. With garlic sauce."

Madeline added, "Get a chicken dish. Or duck."

Kimmy pointed to the menu and said, "Crispy duck. This one."

"Something green, too. Gotta eat something green," Sya said.

Madeline smiled.

She tried to instill in Sya a love of vegetables. "One green every day," she always insisted.

"Chinese broccoli, Hong Kong style," Kimmy said in her perfect Chinese.

Another waiter poured water and smiled at Kimmy.

Madeline picked up her bag and pulled out a neatly arranged folder.

"Your father put this folder together for us. In preparation for this trip. He's had it organized for a very long time. Way before he..."

Madeline wept.

Sam's death took a toll on her emotional stability, and she found it difficult to even reflect on any element of her past that involved Sam.

Kimmy sensed a distinct sadness coming over the table.

"Mrs. P., have you ever heard about the dragon boat festival here in Hong Kong? It's a reason for us to come back again."

Sya picked up a photo from the folder and handed it to Madeline.

"Is this me?

Still shaking, Madeline unintentionally dropped the photo.

Sya picked it up off the floor, not knowing what to make of Madeline's reaction. She found herself often confused by Madeline in the way she responded to things.

"Look, a map. Here's the hotel. The orphanage. It's not too far away."

"Well, definitely too far to walk. We'll just take a taxi. Are you sure you still want to go through with this?" Madeline said.

"What are you so afraid of?" Sya said.

The waiter interrupted the conversation with the steamed fish appetizer.

Kimmy pushed her fork in the fish nearest to her.

"I'm diggin' in. No one has to wait for me."

Madeline quickly changed the topic.

"You're all I have now."

Kimmy, with food in her mouth, said, "Hey, you have me too, Mrs. P."

"Don't talk with food in your mouth, Kimmy. Manners."

Madeline positioned her chopstick to flip over the fish.

"I just want this to be over."

"Don't flip it. Don't flip the fish," Kimmy said.

"Yeh, they say it's bad luck," Sya added.

Madeline stopped and didn't flip the fish. She wanted nothing to change her luck.

Wulan Orphanage

Sya and Kimmy ran ahead of Madeline and stood before the large wooden double doors with the ornamental brass knockers. Kimmy confirmed with Sya that the Chinese characters above the door read Wulan. Sya stared at the word orphanage under the Chinese characters and stood motionless. She laid her hand flat on the wooden door and closed her eyes. This place was her home and part of her story.

She took a deep breath, and then reached for the massive doorknocker. It was cold and reminded her of when she touched Sam's nose in the casket at the funeral home. She wished he were here with them.

"Kimmy, this is it. It's real. We are here. It's about to happen."

She gently put the ring down and stepped back, hesitating one last time before she knocked. She knew that this door would open a chapter to her past. And, while she had always yearned for this very moment, she couldn't help but feel fear and trepidation. This was the first time that she questioned whether she would be able to process so many sensory inputs during this visit.

Kimmy bobbled around Sya teasing her with the cadence of her request.

"This is it, my sis'. What's holding you back, dear, dear girl? Come, on. Knock. Knock."

Madeline stood a few steps behind Sya and Kimmy. She remembered the first time she knocked on these very doors. Sam held her in his arms as he peered into her tear-stained eyes. He assured her that they were on this journey together and that their little girl was on the other side of these doors waiting to be held and loved by them.

She remembered the knot in her stomach and the dogs barking as the midday sun warmed their faces. There could be no other feelings as intense as the ones she felt that day. She was joyful, afraid, worried, wound-up, and exhausted.

Could she take care of a baby?

Would she be a good mother?

Was she cut out to be a mother at all?

Would she know what to do?

Was this something that she could handle?

Was it the right decision?

Those voices came back louder than ever as she stared at the orphanage door. Madeline stood at the apex of uncertainty.

Sya's aggressive knock on the door brought Madeline back into the moment. The sound echoed through the alley.

They stood and waited.

The door to the orphanage opened slowly.

A Chinese woman with a bright smile and eyes tight from worry and sadness stuck her head out of the door and peered downward to the right side of the door stoop.

She carried a large ring of keys that were dangling at her waist. They made a clunking sound as she leaned forward as if to reach for something not there.

Sya turned her head left and looked down on the step where the woman had set her gaze.

"Hello, ma'am. What are you looking for?" Sya asked.

"Babies. Mostly girl babies. Usually right here. On the step."

Girl toddlers peeked around the door and pulled at the woman's dress, drawing her into the orphanage.

She reached out to shake Sya, Kimmy, and Madeline's hand.

"Come in, please. How may I help you?"

The woman motioned to the three of them to enter. As they did, they could hear a variety of baby sounds, gleeful sounds of small children, and music echoing throughout the compound.

Sya and Kimmy stood in amazement. The building, though old, was grand, and had an airy front portico, high ceilings, an ornate staircase, and an enclosed Garden of Eden-like courtyard filled with plants. The children in the courtyard played with Xin Xin, a large German shepherd dog, who was the star of the fun.

Sya wrinkled her nose.

"What's that smell?"

Madeline looked at Sya and mouthed the word "bleach."

After the woman let them in, she turned around and locked the door.

"Keeps them in and keeps them out."

Sya locked eyes with many of the girls. Each one connected for a brief moment, then looked away.

"So many girls."

The woman escorted Sya, Madeline, and Kimmy through the long orphanage hallways.

"Help me to recall, are you here exploring adoption?" she said.

Madeline answered first.

"Well, we want..."

"A boy, no doubt? Sorry, we only have girls. Few boys ever see this place. Can't help you with a boy. They keep the boys, you know. We specialize in girls, beautiful little girls."

"Oh, no we don't want a boy. We are not here to adopt," Madeline said.

"My manners. I'm Director Chu. This way."

"Madeline. Madeline Porter. Were you the one I spoke with about our arrival?

"Yes."

The children distracted Sya, and she bent down to interact with them.

The woman directed her question to Sya.

"And, what's your name?"

Madeline nudged Sya to stand up and address Director Chu.

"Sorry. Sya Cynee' Porter."

"Pleased to meet you Sya Cynee' – is that how you say it? Did you know Sya is of Chinese origin? It means summer. I don't believe that I've heard this name Cynee' before? Is that a family name?"

Sya paused to look at Madeline with big eyes as if to request that she answer the question.

Madeline gave her big eyes back.

Sya continued. "I'm named after a famous reporter in Washington, DC. Her name was Cynee' Simpson. A TV reporter. She was my mom's favorite news person."

Madeline smiled.

"Director Chu, we wanted to see if…"

Madeline looked at Sya, then at Director Chu.

Sya froze.

"I came here to find my parents. My birth parents. I was here. At Wulan. Do you remember me?"

"I'm sorry, Sya. I don't remember you. Perhaps I wasn't here when you were. And, since I've been here, we've arranged so many adoptions. Thousands."

"Kinda like selling cattle, huh."

Sya's response shocked Madeline.

"Sya!"

The conversation was interrupted by the sound of Chinese instruments.

"What's that sound? It's beautiful and haunting at the same time," Sya said as she tried to change the subject.

Director Chu led Sya and Madeline to a large room where eight animated blind girls were playing Chinese instruments.

The mini-concert sound and the musical blend drew them in.

Kimmy walked over to the larger instrument.

"This is a guzheng."

Sya was mesmerized by what she saw and bent closer to the strings to watch.

"Wow. Just wow. I'd love to learn how to play this."

"These were donated by the American Embassy. Each Chinese New Year for about 15 years, they have provided us with several new instruments."

Sya walked closer to the girls. They sensed her presence and played with more energy. Very seldom did they have an audience that expressed so much interest.

A well-dressed, well-mannered, and handsome Chinese boy in his mid-teens, who looked like he didn't belong in an orphanage with all girls, stood in the doorway watching the exchange and staring at Kimmy. He coyly smiled at her. She smiled back as she flipped her red hair over her right shoulder.

Kimmy felt the chemistry between the two of them but was interrupted by Director Chu who shooed the boy out of the room.

Disappointed, Kimmy turned to Director Chu and said, "I thought you said you didn't have boys in here."

"We don't. That is my son. The International School is on holiday."

"As I was saying, we have strong community support for our music program," Director Chu added.

Sya and Madeline sat down to listen.

Curious, Kimmy hovered around the instrumentalists.

Sya closed her eyes and swayed side to side. The music mesmerized her. As she leaned forward, her necklace charm on the gold chain, fell out of her shirt, and hung perpendicular to the ground.

Director Chu transfixed her gaze on the gold heart necklace, and her rosy cheeks descended slowly.

Madeline sensed her change in demeanor. Uncomfortable with what she had just witnessed, Madeline tried to interrupt Director Chu's stare.

"Director Chu, how long have you been here?"

Director Chu looked up and locked eyes with Madeline, creating an uncomfortable moment.

"Ten or so years. Over 30,000 adoptions. Your name again? What's your last name?"

Madeline was puzzled by her behavior.

"Porter. Madeline Porter. Sam and I came...Sam, my husband, he passed away earlier this year...Sam and I adopted Sya here in 1990. When she was three."

"Why don't you tour the orphanage while I get your file? Xiaoyuan?"

"Yes, Madam."

"Can you take Mrs. Porter, Sya, and Kimmy Lancaster on the tour?"

Director Chu hurriedly left the room and walked to her office.

Xiaoyuan, Sya, Kimmy, and Madeline walked the opposite direction. They passed many rooms with girl children. In one room, thirty small bamboo cribs housed girl infants. Some of the cribs held two children.

The crying children created a wall of sound that was nearly unbearable.

Madeline reached for Sya's hand to gauge her reaction before she spoke to Xiaoyuan.

"Is it like this all the time?" Madeline asked.

Xiaoyuan shook her head no.

"Low, low tide," she said

Fiona, a feisty, but extremely dedicated Australian volunteer, and Qiao, a young and timid Chinese nurse assistant busily prepared formula for the children. One by one, they propped bottles on towels so that the babies could eat unattended.

"Tricks of the trade," Fiona retorted as she waved them out.

"Feeding time. Out. Out! Well, unless you're here to help out. And from the looks of those faces, that is not the case."

Her manner startled Sya, Kimmy, and Madeline, who backed out of the room in response to her brusque command.

Xiaoyuan, who knew better than to cross paths with Fiona, waited outside the room and watched the exchange.

She intercepted Sya, Kimmy, and Madeline as they came out into the hallway.

"This way. Good and bad. Fiona. Good and bad."

She guided them down the hallway near the courtyard by a group of rambunctious teenage girls who giggled and exhibited apparent disdain for Xiaoyuan.

Madeline watched Xiaoyuan's top lip curl up and to the left as she grit her teeth. Xiaoyuan had the face of a mistreated bulldog that had not been fed in a while.

Madeline stepped out of her way and pulled Sya with her.

Xiaoyuan pointed toward the back of the building and in Chinese told the girls to leave the hallway and go to the courtyard.

The girls ran off looking back at the group and laughing disrespectfully at Xiaoyuan.

Xiaoyuan turned to Madeline.

"They need be removed," Xiaoyuan said in her broken English.

"Removed?"

Sya joined the conversation.

"To where?"

"Factories."

Out of fear, Madeline pulls Sya and Kimmy away from Xiaoyuan.

Kimmy turned around for a brief moment and noticed that Director Chu's son had watched the whole exchange from the other side of the courtyard.

She was the only one that noticed him.

She flashed her toothy grin.

He smiled back.

As Sya and Madeline left the courtyard and started walking down the hallway, Kimmy stayed behind and walked past the fountain in the courtyard to interact with Director Chu's son.

In Chinese, Kimmy asked the boy his name.

He smiled at her.

He reached out to touch her flaming red hair.

Speaking in his best English, he said, "Oh, a red-haired, blue-eyed girl who also speaks Chinese? You first."

Kimmy curtsied and continued speaking in Chinese.

"My name is Kimmy Lancaster. Ever so pleased to meet you."

Clearing the Dust

Dilapidated filing cabinets from the 1940s filled the large, dusty file room. The dented sides of the cabinets bent slightly outward and rust coated the handles and parts of the drawer faces. Very few of the drawers could be opened or closed with ease. Many wore faded or partially removed labels.

Standing before a drawer labeled 1990 – N, O, and P, Director Chu struggled to pull the drawer out. Apparently, no one had opened it for some time. She yanked it so hard, she and the drawer fell to the floor. She chuckled and pulled herself up.

She frantically thumbed through the "P" folders and mumbled to herself as she stirred up the dust that had settled on them.

"P. Po. Por. Porter."

Director Chu found the file she was looking for, held it to her chest, and shut her eyes.

She was startled when she heard someone walking down the hallway, so she quickly walked to the back of the filing room to hide. She placed the folder on a small table, hidden from view.

She paced back and forth scratching her forehead.

"This is Guli. Is this Guli? This is Guli. Is this girl my baby?"

Director Chu sounded like she was plucking the petals of a flower and calling the "he loves me, he loves me not" chant. Afraid, she picked up the folder again but didn't look in it. She put the folder back down and paced again as she mumbled to herself.

Hesitating, she stepped outside the file room and looked both ways. The hallway was quiet. There was no reason for her not to open the folder. She had every right to open the folder, and in reality, it didn't matter if anyone saw her do it.

She hesitated.

Her fear took control of her behavior and her thoughts.

She backed into the room and sat on the dusty, red velvet dining chair, a donation from the American Embassy. She shopped at the same market as the Ambassador's secretary, Sally, and was on speaking terms with her. Because of this, she got many of the embassy's hand-me-downs.

She took a deep breath and slowly opened the folder. She found the Wulan intake form she was looking for: Madeline and Sam Porter, 1731 Gough St., Baltimore, MD 21231. Director Chu noticed in the top right of the page in all capital letters: "FIVE KNOCKS."

Stapled to the top of the intake form was a copy of a handwritten note. She stared at it.

"This cannot be," she thought. "Is this the note that I wrote so many years ago?"

She pulled the note to her chest and cried large tears.

Director Chu bit her bottom lip as her breathing became shallow. She found it difficult to control her emotions and her thoughts. Her mind raced. She remembered that day well. She still carried the pain of that day, and while she felt an emotional rawness inside, she still harbored the hope that one day she would meet her daughter again to explain everything.

The texture of the paper in her hands also brought her a moment of happiness, as she knew that this might lead her closer to her daughter, whose memory she held dear and recalled each day of her life.

She read the note aloud in Chinese, stopped for a moment, then closed her eyes. The pain was almost too much for her to bear.

"My baby daughter. Born July 26..."

Director Chu remembered in exquisite details of the day Guli was born. She could still feel the harshness of the over starched bed sheets, smell the odd hospital smells, and choke on the penetrating bleach odor of the maternity ward.

Her heart beat faster as she remembered Chu Shang's reaction when Guli was born.

"A maggot in the rice," he said.

So cruel, she thought. That he could say something so mean was unthinkable. The sadness she felt remained resident in her being and reminded her of the hate that she still harbored for Chu Shang. She forced herself to put aside those thoughts, but she was never good at doing so.

That One We Keep

Chu Shang, an aggressive and angry-at-the-world man, paced the sanitarium hallway with the stiffness of an uptight, high-ranking Chinese government official. It was 1987. He still held the lead population scientist position in Deng Xiaoping's cabinet. He was part of Deng's "drinking buddy" inner circle, and full eyewitness to and an active player in the fundamental reforms being put in place to transform China.

Chu Shang, the author of China's one-child policy, held a key position in the maelstrom of coercion and deceit. He was the last person in the world that needed to have a wife pregnant with two girls. For the entirety of Chu Meiying's pregnancy, Chu Shang cloistered his wife from family and friends feigning a contagious illness. In the latter part of her pregnancy, Meiying's doctor told them that she was carrying twin girls. With that news, they traveled to Hong Kong to hide the birth of their girl children, and as he put it, "take care of their little problem" before his colleagues or Deng found out about their policy-breaking circumstance.

In their first day in the Hong Kong hospital, Chu Shang admonished Meiying, who was in labor, as if the gender of the children was her fault.

"Get this over, quickly," he said.

"Shang, don't blame me. I had no control over the sex of these babies, and we..."

"Meiying, we must control the story. You were never pregnant. There are no babies. Hong Kong is the perfect place to hide this and get rid of the problem," he said.

Meiying screamed from the labor pains.

"Get out."

Chu Shang pushed a nurse away from the bed and rammed his face into Meiying's.

"Count on it. This will never happen again," he said.

Meiying slapped him across the face, as she pushed her first baby out. A girl.

"A maggot in the rice," Chu Shang said in disgust.

He turned away and walked to the door.

The nurse stared at Chu Shang in disgust as Meiying silently struggled to give life to her second child. With one last push, the baby arrived.

The silence in the room was deafening.

Meiying had given birth to a boy.

Nothing could explain the feelings and the emotions Meiying felt at that moment. She had expected two girls. She had already prepared herself to walk out of the hospital with no children.

Now, she and Chu Shang had a son. She wanted to feel a sense of excitement but was already feeling the loss and the dread of having to give up her baby girl.

Expressionless, the nurse turned toward Chu Shang and announced, "Boy."

Shocked, Chu Shang turned around, and rushed to the bed to confirm the announcement.

"That one, we keep," he said.

The Red Envelope

Meiying, still in the hospital bed, held the day-old babies in her arms as she breastfed them. She positioned the baby girl on her right and the boy on her left. She allowed herself to fantasize about and look forward to her zuo yuezi, that month-long focused time with her two children.

She had so many dreams for them. But, that's what they were. Dreams. She needed to prepare herself for the inevitable. There wouldn't be two children in her future. Chu Shang had already laid down the law. She did everything in her power to relish and fully experience the moment.

With her babies suckling at her breasts, she glanced at each of them knowing that she needed to etch this scene in her memory.

"I'm a mother. These are my children. This very moment may cease to exist and never repeat itself. Ever," she thought.

At the doorway of the room, Chu Shang talked in a hushed whisper to the attending nurse. She watched as he discreetly handed the nurse a thick red envelope. He then turned to Meiying and pointed to the baby on her right side.

"Get rid of it."

The nurse left the room without taking the baby.

Chu Shang walked into the room and paced with his back to Meiying. The one-child policy had come to rest in her house and with her family.

"Shang, is there another way?" she asked.

"I'm a senior population scientist with Deng at my neck. You, more than anyone, know that we must follow this policy that I created. One child per couple. Be happy. With one."

"Why must we choose, Shang? Governments should not tell families how many children they..."

Chu Shang raced to the bed and forced Meiying's shoulders down and slapped her face. The babies pulled away from her breasts and cried. Her upper lip bled from the blunt force of his wedding ring.

Feeling overwhelmed by the hate in her heart, she looked up at Chu Shang and spat the blood that had pooled in her mouth.

She had never done anything like that before.

She was a good Chinese wife.

An obedient wife.

A polite wife.

A wife who never spoke up.

A wife who knew her place.

A wife who served.

A wife who quietly watched.

A wife who was safer in the shadows.

A wife who was an outsider to her own marriage.

She clenched her teeth with the power of a Rottweiler and pulled her upper and lower lips together like she was closing a drawstring bag. In that moment, she felt dominant and powerful for the first time in her life. She liked that feeling.

Chu Shang stood near the bed in shock as he pulled the bed sheet cover to wipe the blood off of his face and shirt. He pierced her with his stare, as the babies cried louder and flailed in the bed.

"It's for China," he said in anger.

"For you, Shang. Don't forget that. For you. You benefited from this deal."

"We, and my beloved son, benefited from the deal."

Meiying turned her head away. She wondered where she fit in. Was she merely just the vehicle for giving him a son?

"OK. I see. I'm just a bystander."

Chu Shang slapped Meiying's face again.

She yelled, "What we'll never understand is the toll this one-child policy has on everyone. The mothers. The girls who are abandoned. The only sons. This will surely change the fabric of our society. You will live to regret this decision."

As he stormed out of the room, he yelled back at her. "That is not for our concern. Change was necessary."

After Chu Shang left the room, she struggled to get out of the bed. Her body hurt from the pain of childbirth. She struggled with the weight of the two babies as she placed them in the cribs beside her bed.

She walked back to the nightstand and opened up the drawer. She had placed a small box with two beautiful gold necklaces, each matching designs, inside the drawer.

When Meiying had her first ultrasound, the doctors told her that she was expecting two daughters. She had purchased a necklace for each daughter.

The front side of each necklace was a three-dimensional "flower in a cage" heart-shaped design. One side was flat, and the other looked like a beautiful, weaved fence. The Chinese character for daughter adorned the back of each heart.

Two girls. Two gold necklaces.

Now, she would only mark one child as she handed off that baby to a stranger whose task was to get rid of it.

Meiying had only minutes to ready her baby girl before the nurse took the baby away. Her face tensed, her eyes watered, and she could feel her body begin to shake to her core.

Meiying held dear a profound wish that her girl child would not face an ugly fate just because she was born a girl. Maybe, just maybe, she thought, her baby would end up in the arms of another woman who would give her the love that she needed to thrive.

She also experienced a sense of gratitude from the fact that she was in Hong Kong and not China for the birth of her babies. If in China, she may have experienced forced abortion or a home invasion if Chinese officials found out that she was carrying two girl children.

She removed one of the necklaces and placed it in a small pink silk purse.

She reached for a pen and paper in the drawer and hurriedly wrote the following message in Chinese characters: "My baby girl, Chu Guli. Born July 26, 1989, at 7:38 p.m. With this act, I suffer great shame and sadness. Your father chose to keep your twin brother. Tradition never dies. Neither will my love for you. I pray you have a good life. Mother, Meiying.

She tucked the paper and the necklace in the purse and stuffed it out of sight deep into Guli's swaddling. She picked up both babies and struggled to position them again for what would be Guli's last breastfeeding.

With a twin in each arm, Meiying closed her eyes and tried to fall asleep, knowing full well that this day and the memories of this moment would forever haunt her.

She felt swallowed up by the room's darkness and the sadness that filled her small and tired body.

Shortly after, the nurse entered the room and awakened a sleeping Meiying.

It was time to let go.

The nurse reached for the baby girl.

Both were holding the baby when they locked eyes.

"Let her live," Meiying pleaded.

The nurse looked toward the closed door and leaned into Meiying to whisper something.

"Your baby...I bring to Wulan..."

She stopped talking to Meiying and stood erect as Chu Shang burst open the door and marched into the room.

Sensing that the moment needed to be interrupted, he walked to the bed and yanked the girl child away from both of them.

"Out!"

He handed the girl baby to the nurse.

"Go. Now," Chu Shang barked.

The nurse locked eyes again with Meiying and hastily exited the room.

Meiying turned over to her right side and in a cocoon-like fashion, drew her knees to her chest, and curled her body around the boy in her bed.

Nothing could explain the emptiness that she felt.
Chu Shang got the boy he so desperately wanted.
Her baby girl was gone.

Not a Game

Director Chu removed the note and placed the forms into the folder. She paced with the note in her hand. She looked at it and paced again. She carefully folded the note and reached to put it back in the folder. She stopped, and then put the note in her pocket.

Wiping the tears from her eyes, she stiffened her posture and with the folder in her hand, headed back to her office. She unlocked the door and walked to her desk.

As she was about to sit down, Xiaoyuan, Sya, and Madeline entered her office.

"Is that from my adoption?" Sya asked.

Director Chu looked up from the folder.

"Yes. Please have a seat."

She motioned Xiaoyuan to leave the office and to shut the door on her way out.

Still standing, Director Chu again noticed Sya's necklace.

"That's a beautiful necklace, Sya."

"Thank you."

Madeline chimed in.

"When we adopted Sya, the orphanage staff told us that they found the necklace inside a small pink silk purse that had been tucked in her clothing. They gave us the necklace, but for some reason, they didn't give us the pink purse."

Director Chu sat down at her desk.

"Your mother...she must have loved you."

"My mother?"

Puzzled and frustrated by the statement, Sya responded, "Yeh, uh, loved me enough to abandon me."

Visibly hurt by Sya's words, Director Chu averted her eyes to the floor in shame. Madeline noticed her reaction.

"Do you know what the character on the back side of the charm means?" Director Chu asked.

Sya turned over the charm, which had been facing inward the whole time.

"No," she said.

Before Director Chu could answer, they were distracted by the clamor and yelling outside of Director Chu's office windows that opened directly to the courtyard.

Director Chu breathed deeply and felt relieved by the distraction.

A group of noisy girls hovered around the open windows, laughing, chanting in Chinese, and chasing one another.

"They seem so happy," Sya said.

After a brief moment, Sya looked again at Director Chu and pointed to the folder.

"Anything about my birth parents in there?"

Director Chu shuffled through the pages.

"I'm afraid that..."

Sya's impatience became overbearing, and her voice showed her frustration.

"Afraid that what? Tell me something. Come on. Tell me anything."

Director Chu hesitated again.

Madeline added to Sya's questioning.

"Please, is there anything? Give us one thing. Anything. Please."

Director Chu knew that she had to give them something.

"The only thing noteworthy here is on this form. It says, FIVE KNOCKS."

Frustrated with the lack of information, Sya responded, "Five knocks? What the heck does that mean? Five knocks?"

"Girl babies are delivered to Wulan on a regular basis. We know that it's the same person. Whoever it is knocks on the orphanage door five times. When we hear that, we know that there will be child left on our doorstep. We try to get to the door in time to see who it is, but whoever it is runs away before we open the door. You were delivered by that person to Wulan."

Exasperated, Sya sat down and hung her head.

"Five knocks. What a clue. What can we do with that clue? Shall we try to track this person down? Sit by the door, and wait for the knock. Then when we hear it, open the door quickly to see whom this 'five knocks' person is? Even if we caught up with this person, would he or she know anything about my parents? It's been so long ago. This seems so hopeless."

As Director Chu reached in her pocket for the note, the teenage girls in the courtyard burst out laughing again.

Director Chu stood up slowly and shut the window to remove the distraction.

Overcome by the bad news, Sya turned to Madeline.

Director Chu could hardly bare Sya's reaction. She placed her hand on her heart as she said, "I wish I had different news for you, Sya."

Sya's lip quivered.

"What are you not telling us?"

"I can only tell you that you're a victim of a policy that has destroyed the lives of innocent Chinese girls and the lives of the parents who..."

She paused and stared down at her desk as she said: "The parents who abandon them."

The girls' activity in the courtyard drew Madeline's attention again.

"So many girls without a home," Madeline said.

Sya watched two of them on her left jumping around like ants were trying to bite their feet. They laughed and screamed as they took turns clapping their hands in between their jumps.

"How can they be so happy?" Sya asked.

"We teach our girls that gender is not a liability. We give them a strong sense of self," Director Chu said.

Sya continued her line of questioning.

"How do you help them get rid of that feeling of being rejected? Abandoned. No. Kicked aside."

"Sya! Back off a bit here," Madeline scolded.

"Well, think about it. I'm nothing more than an over quota girl. A victim of a stupid policy. A victim of blatant sexism."

Sya and Director Chu's eyes locked.

Sya turned away and focused her attention again on the girls outside of the window.

Madeline stared at Director Chu, and cocked her head to the right in a quizzical fashion as if to say, "What was that all about?"

"What can be done here?" she blurted out to Director Chu as if she had the power to do something about it.

Director Chu readied herself for the line of questioning she experienced so many times before with parents who came back to the orphanage with their daughters. She often thought about what one person could and should say in this kind of circumstance.

"If we criticize the government, it only makes our job more difficult. So, we just do our best. But, all of the orphanages are at capacity. In China and in Hong Kong. This situation pushes many families to take desperate actions. This policy is at the center of a host of many problems for China. Rampant abortion. Infanticide. Hong Kong receives a lot of China's abandoned children. The orphanages and the streets. The lucky ones make it here."

As Director Chu spouted what seemed like a response that she had used many times before, Sya interrupted her.

"I don't know what lucky feels like. Tell me."

"Well, Sya, we work hard to give the girls a chance to be in a family so that they can live a better life, in a better place than here."

"It seems like a prison here."

"We are making the most of a bad situation," Director Chu said.

Sya reached for Madeline's hands.

"Can we go now? I can't take this anymore."

Sya burst into tears and ran out of Director Chu's office.

Madeline stood up and reached for Sya.

"Sya, wait!"

She followed her down the hallway.

"Young lady, come, here, now. Did you have to be so cruel? That woman hasn't done anything to you. I don't appreciate your behavior. People have feelings. You don't even know this person, and you're acting as if she's done something wrong to you. I thought I taught you better than that. Have a little respect, please!"

Madeline coiled back when she realized that her voice was too loud on that last statement. The marble floors carried her voice nearly to the front door of the orphanage.

Fiona, a brusque-sounding volunteer with a heart of gold, approached Sya and Madeline.

"Hate to butt into such a, um, nice conversation, however..."

Sya felt like she was getting it from all sides.

"Look, lady I don't need another lecture."

"Feisty one, aren't you? Your mother's right, you know."

"She's not my mother. I mean, well, not my birth mother."

Sya looked at Madeline.

Hurt, Madeline stared back at Sya. A blank stare embedded with so much meaning. Her face reflected a deep sadness that Sya had never seen before.

"I'm sorry. I didn't mean it that way," Sya said.

She could tell that Madeline was cracking at the seams.

Madeline turned away from the two of them and walked back toward Director Chu's office.

"Oh, that's swell, little lady. Not your mother, huh? I overheard what you said earlier about not knowing what lucky feels like. You don't think you're lucky? You live in a free country. Have choices. You were chosen. You have a family...You have a mother who brought you all the way here to find your birth parents. Many of these girls will never be adopted and loved and taken care of like you. You're lucky. Did you mean to hurt her?"

"No."

"Well, you did. Girlie, you just don't know how lucky you are."

"Sorry."

"No need to tell me you're sorry. That's not where sorry goes. Look here, treat your mother better than that. She's the only real mother you have. While your mom's doing that, come to our gift shop. Not much to offer, but will take your mind off of what you just did."

Madeline entered Director Chu's office.

"I'm sorry, Director Chu. She so badly wants to find her parents. To connect with them at least once. I'll admit it's a drive that's unmatched. She's obsessed with it to a fault."

Director Chu stood up, walked to the door, looked both ways down the hallway, and slowly closed it.

"What I'm about to tell you...you must not ask me any questions."

"Ok, don't get all mysterious on me here. What are you talking about?"

"There is something more important than Sya's search for her parents," Director Chu said.

"Look, lady, you don't know my daughter. She's dreamt of meeting her birth parents her whole life. No matter what I do. No matter what I give to her. Not that I can give her that much. I'm a single parent with a shit-paying job, living in a lower, middle-class neighborhood with rats in my attic. It's a miracle we are even here today. If it weren't for my husband saving for three years, this trip here never would've happened. There's a hole in my little girl's heart. Can't you understand that? Nothing can fill it. Not me. Not you. Not anyone."

"Madeline, I've been waiting for this day."

"You've been waiting for this day?"

"Oh, my dear Madeline," she said as she handed her Sya's folder with the small pink purse on the inside.

"Please let me explain," Director Chu said.

Dead End

After Sya finished her visit to the gift shop, she paced the hallways exploring the rooms in the orphanage. In every one she passed, she paused and peered into the doorway. She saw rail thin babies, babies with deformities, babies sleeping in high chairs with their heads bent forward looking as if their airways were blocked.

All girls.

So many girls.

She followed the labyrinthine hallways, exploring a reality that was hers, but she remembered little of the experience.

Hyperventilating, she fought back her tears.

This was part of her past.

This was her home.

Checking first to see that no one was around, she entered the room with about thirty baby cribs. Going row by row, she walked around each crib, looking at the sleeping babies. Dizzy from what she saw, she paused for a moment and stuck her head inside of one crib. She made a clicking sound with her tongue as she touched the rosy cheeks of the three babies looking up at her.

They cooed. It made her smile.

Fiona entered the room and startled her.

"Excuse me, little lady. You shouldn't be in here."

"Sorry. Just curious."

"Why? You want one?"

"No."

Standing frozen behind the crib, Sya waited for the next question.

"You want to have a normal conversation?" Fiona asked.

Sya nods yes.

"What brings you to Wulan?"

"My search. For my birth parents."

"Yeh, you and 1 million other Chinese girls."

"Did you say one mill..."

"Look, sweetie, don't waste your time. Twenty dollars to a hat pin, you'll never find them."

Sya walked toward Fiona.

"You're not very helpful. Or hopeful."

"Just realistic, little lady. Treasure what you have."

Sya honestly felt that there was something refreshing about Fiona's frankness, but she wasn't ready to confront a reality defined by Fiona. She still carried an earnest hope that she would find her parents.

Sya walked backward out of the room, then raced toward Director Chu's office. Four hours had passed. Sya was ready to leave.

She stood next to Director Chu's closed office door and tried to peer through the crack in the door to determine if Madeline was still in the office. She could hear voices.

"Mama?"

Inside, both Madeline and Director Chu turned to face the door. They answered Sya in unison.

"Yes."

Director Chu's jaw stiffened as Sya swung open the door and raced toward Madeline.

Crying, Sya hugged Madeline.

"Let's get out of here. This is a big dead end."

Sya walked out of the office down the hallway as Madeline picked up her things in Director Chu's office. As she exited, Madeline turned around and looked back at Director Chu one last time in a state of shock.

Director Chu mouthed the words, "She must never know."

Speaking of Money

Sya and Kimmy always got a kick out of jogging in the heavy rain. They both loved getting hit in the face by big raindrops and made it a point to call each other for a run when there was a steady Baltimore downpour.

Sya typically ran about 20 yards in front of Kimmy. On this day, they had been running for about four miles when a blue Toyota Prius driven by a college-aged, handsome Chinese young man pulled up beside Kimmy and waved as he drove past. He had followed them for the last mile. Kimmy waved back as he sped away.

Sya maintained her speed and didn't notice as the car passed her. They continued to run and neared the spot where the motorbike hit Sam. Sya paused from physical and emotional exhaustion.

"Can we stop?"

"Sure."

"It seems like yesterday we were here watching my dad die. He was my biggest supporter, you know. And all the money in the world can't bring him back."

"Speaking of money."

"Really, Kimmy."

"Sorry."

"OK, what? What about money? Where are you going with this?"

"I mean, I don't wanna seem like a nosy Nellie here, or anything like that, but uh, I just need to ask. What's changed with you, Sya?"

"What are you talking about?"

"I mean, what's changed with your family situation? You buy the best. You wear the best. You've got more jewelry than the Queen of England."

"And?"

"Come on. You used to live in a row house, and you were one of us girls. Bam. One of us."

"A poor girl. Is that what you're saying, Kimmy? A poor girl."

"Not poor, but sometimes...how do I say this...um, a girl without much. You had less allowance than we did. Now, look at you. For, example." Kimmy said as she pointed to Sya's double row diamond tennis bracelet.

"That."

Then, she reached for Sya's 9-diamond dinner ring.

"And this."

Sya pulled away.

"And, you wear all of this running. I don't know. Seems a bit reckless."

"Kimmy. What are you trying to say?"

"Did all this come from your Dad's life insurance? I mean, I don't wanna get into your personal business, but..."

"So don't."

"Sorry."

"I don't know. I don't know. I mean. Never thought about it. Not really. I see something I want. I get it. I like buying. Unfettered buying."

"Yeh, and what full-blooded American doesn't?"

Sya glared at her, but only for a moment.

"My mother never says no, Kimmy."

"So, the well just never runs dry?"

"I don't ask questions. Not sure I want to. Don't they say that sometimes it's best not to know the truth."

"Wait a second. I'm gonna call you on that. Haven't you dedicated your life to finding truth?"

"Selective perception. Selective recall."

"Maybe that needs to change, don't you think, Sya?"

"Or maybe I've given up."

Kimmy didn't believe Sya for a second.

"Doubt that."

Sya couldn't stand the pressure.

"When did you think you had the right to get all up in my business?" Sya asked.

"Yup, it's late," as she raced away.

"Last one back to your house buys beer Friday after the JHU Chinese dragon performance," Kimmy yelled.

Excess and Secrets

You could call it a girly room. Lots of pink. Too many things for one child. Collector Barbies, Cabbage Patch dolls, Beanie Babies, electronics, a Mac laptop computer, a Mac desktop computer, an iPad, and an iPhone. Expensive Asian art graced the walls. A Chinese pipa leaned against a 1000-gallon aquarium filled with many exotic and colorful fish. The room held the fineries of a museum.

Sya stood with her hands holding the top of the aquarium and her eyes transfixed on a large, graceful pajama cardinal fish.

Her iPod stereo system played Michael Bublé's "You Are Always On My Mind."

The blue light beams, reflecting through the water, wrapped around her tiny frame and created a shimmering effect on her long, black hair.

A large stack of textbooks and notebooks sat to the right of the aquarium. On her desk, there were eight books about adoption. Just above the desk, pages of articles about finding your birth parents graced a bulletin board that was devoted to all things adoption: "How to Find Your Birth Parents Without Hiring An Agency;" "What Adopted Children Wish Their Parents Knew;" "Reach Out! Making a Decision to Find Your Birth Parents;" and "Missing Birth Parents."

The clicking sound of Madeline's high heels tapping on the marble floor interrupted Sya's thoughts.

Madeline knocked and entered Sya's room.

Sya ignored her. She picked up the box of fish food, and walked to the back of the aquarium, and poured a bit of food in the left corner.

Madeline moved about the room like a hummingbird searching for nectar.

She straightened the desk.

She adjusted the art on the wall.

She picked up the books off of the floor.

Her movement was in stark contrast to a near motionless Sya.

Sya continued to stare at the pajama cardinalfish.

"Stop already," Sya said to Madeline.

"I just love the pink polka dots on this fish. Did you give him a name yet?" Madeline asked.

Sya leaned her head back and looked at the ceiling for a moment thinking that if her mother really knew her, she would already know that all of her fish had names.

"They all have names," Sya said.

"This one? What is it?" Madeline asked.

Sya played along.

"Matteo."

Madeline never understood Sya's reasoning, but she always had a story or rationale to justify the names. She grabbed a tissue and started cleaning the aquarium glass.

Sya plopped herself on the bed thinking, "Here she goes again."

Their conversation mimicked the cadence and rhythm of the dueling banjos in the Devil and Daniel Webster's song.

"A place name? You named it after San Mateo, California."

"Mom, it's M-a-t-t-e-o. Two t's, not one," Sya said.

Madeline straightened up the bed.

"OK. I'll get it. Give me minute. Hmm. It's coming to me. Yes. The convent. The Convent of San Matteo. In Italy. Where Galileo sent his illegitimate daughter. That one is two 't's."

"Nope. Good guess."

"OK Sya, here's my third and final answer. Jesuit priest. The guy who created the first maps in China. Matteo Ricci."

"Uggghhh. History freak."

"You're the one that named the fish. Maybe I should have studied history?"

"What would you do with a history degree?" Sya asked.

"Well, I could be a museum curator," she said as she looked around the room.

Madeline turned off Michael Bublé.

"OK. Why'd ya do that?" Sya asked.

Madeline reached for the pipa, sat on the bed, and then plucked the strings.

The melancholy sound reverberated throughout the room. The marble floors further amplified the sound.

Madeline played louder. Not any particular song, just plucking the strings in a discordant way.

She was clearly trying to annoy Sya.

"Please, don't forget. The dragon dance performance is tomorrow. It's the Wulan Orphanage adoptee reunion night. Will you go with me?"

"Why do you need to go to that?" Madeline asked.

"Look, if you don't want to help me. Don't. I'll do this on my own."

Madeline slammed the instrument on the floor, and the neck separated from the body of the instrument. She didn't look back as she stormed out of Sya's room.

"Great, Ms. Fixer, you sure know how to break things."

Sya heard the sound of Madeline's heels tapping the marble floor and covered her ears. She couldn't stand that sound. It evoked memories of her time at the Wulan Orphanage.

Sya had experienced a strong sensory sensitivity for that sound and attached it to her feelings of physical and emotional abandonment.

She's never told Madeline.

There was a lot Sya had not told Madeline.

There was a lot Madeleine would not tell Sya.

The Small Pink Purse

Sya passed by Madeline's office and noticed one of her desk drawers was slightly open. That drawer piqued her interest. It was usually closed and locked. She listened for Madeline before she quietly entered her office. She pulled the drawer all of the way open. Nothing unusual in the first half of the drawer.

As she ran her fingers across the tops of the file folders, she noticed a beat up folder with frayed edges at the back of the drawer. She leaned forward and tried to make out the letters on the label. The blue ink was smeared.

Sya squinted her eyes to make out the letters. The "l" and the "a" were missing in Wulan, and the "nage" was almost totally smeared off the tab.

Sya's heart raced.

Her palms were sweating.

This was her folder from Wulan Orphanage.

She had never seen it before.

Should she take it out? Should she risk getting caught taking something out of a drawer that her mother always kept locked? She was overwhelmed by the uncertainty she felt.

Sya knew that she must find out what was in this folder. This folder represented her past.

She walked to the office door and peered down the hallway, listening for Madeline. Coast clear.

She returned to the desk and shut the drawer halfway. Then she slid it out all of the way.

She hesitated.

She looked up again and listened for Madeline.

No movement.

She reached for the folder. Holding it by the tattered edges, she slowly pulled the bulging folder out of the drawer. She saw something pink, but she dared not open it.

Sya placed the folder on the desk, careful not to let its contents fall out. She put her outstretched hands atop the folder and rubbed her hands across it as if it were a long-lost friend.

She closed her eyes.

A million questions ran through her head.

Should I open it?

What will I find?

Am I ready for what's in here?

Is this something that my mother has purposefully hidden from me?

Why do I want to know so badly?

Will the information in here make me feel complete?

At that moment, her gag reflex became active, and she had to work hard to keep herself from throwing up. She swallowed to gain her composure.

Meanwhile, Madeline, who had been reading the paper, realized that she had left her desk drawer unlocked. She raced toward her office.

The awful ticking sound of Madeline's heels on the marble floor startled Sya and brought her out of the trance.

Sya knew that she was in trouble. If Madeline had wanted her to see this folder, she would have shared it by now.

She froze.

Madeline entered and stood in the doorway with her arms folded across her chest, her right knee bent, and her right foot resting on top of her left foot.

Sya remained motionless.

Madeline caught her in the act.

She knew Madeline's body language all too well.

Madeline stared at Sya, then stared at the folder. She took a deep breath and drew air through her clenched teeth.

Sya couldn't stand to hear the spit rattle between Madeline's teeth as the air passed through. She knew Madeline was about to lose it.

Sya felt the momentum building and watched as Madeline tried to control and contain her anger. She was good at funneling it into her voice. The sound resembled the high-pitched, hissing sound of a fast-moving torpedo.

Sya swallowed as she tried to protect her ears for what was coming.

Madeline launched into Sya.

"Where did you get that?"

Sya started to cry, and pushed the folder away as she mumbled, "I didn't open it."

Madeline screamed, "Open it. Go ahead. It's what you want to do."

Sya didn't move.

Madeline yelled even louder.

"Open it."

Sya shuddered.

She responded to the command and pulled the folder back toward the edge of the desk. She knew that she had stepped down this rabbit hole, and there was no turning back. She had to open the folder. As she opened it, the small pink silk purse fell on the desk.

Sya looked up to see Madeline's reaction. She stared at the purse, but said nothing.

Sya sat in the office chair and waited for Madeline to respond. Madeline still said nothing. Sya started playing with the pink purse.

"Shall I open it?"

"I'm so sorry. I didn't know how to tell you...I've been meaning to...read it, Sya."

"Meaning to, what? What are you talking about? You know something!"

Sya frantically thumbed through and scanned the papers in the folder. She opened the silk purse and pulled out a small, tattered handwritten note. She struggled to recognize and read the Chinese characters. Her one language class just wasn't enough.

"Baby daughter. July. Seven something, something. This word. It looks like the word brother. Brother? Brother? What the hell?"

"Watch your mouth, young lady."

"Wow. I can't read this one piece of paper that connects me to my past. I'm Chinese, and I can't even read my own language. Sick. Sick. Sick."

Madeline grabbed Sya's hands and pulled her close. She pulled away.

"Wait, can you let me finish? Why do you have to always make it about you? Look at this. Right here. This note is signed Meiying. Her name is Meiying? My mother's name is Meiying? Oh my God."

Madeline hung her head.

"You knew this all along? This paper says that I have a brother. This is my life we're talking about.

"This silk purse and your gold necklace. These were found tucked inside your clothing when you were found on the doorstep of the orphanage," Madeline said.

"When did you get this? Why didn't you tell me before now? You knew my mother's name. Wait. You got this when we visited Wulan. This was the folder that Director Chu had on her desk. She said there were no clues. I don't understand. My whole life has been about finding my parents. I hate you."

Sya didn't stick around for any explanation. She slammed everything off of the desk, aggressively pushed Madeline out of her way, and nearly fell as she frantically tried to get out of the office.

Madeline collapsed amidst the papers on the floor and reached for the small pink purse – the symbol of her promise to Meiying not to say anything to Sya. She didn't know how much longer she would be able to do so.

We Don't Speak Chinese

Sya and Kimmy watched from second-row seats the finale of the Johns Hopkins University (JHU) Yong Han Lion Dance Troupe. The curtains closed, and the audience made its way to the lobby, which filled with Chinese men and women and mixed families with adopted Chinese children.

An annual fundraiser of the Yong Han Lion Dance Troupe and the Baltimore-Chinese School, the event this year was an odd reunion of sorts. The organizers invited families that had adopted Chinese girls from orphanages in Hong Kong and their adopted children. They held the idea that some of the young adults at the event shared a past, and they would find comfort in connecting with each other.

Each adoptee wore a nametag with their adoption year in the upper right-hand corner, their first name, and the name of the orphanage where they were adopted in parentheses. Clusters of Chinese girls started to form.

Sya and Kimmy looked for 1990. They scoured the lobby. Kimmy wove through the crowd ahead of Sya.

"So far, none. I don't see anybody."

"Keep looking."

"Sure thang, Missy," Kimmy said.

"Look, Kimmy. There are two girls over there with 1990 on their nametag. See."

She pointed to the right corner of the room.

"I'm headed there now. What are the chances? I think I can read their nametags. Ya-Shin. Peggy. C'mon, Sya, let's do this." They walked toward Ya-Shin and Peggy.

"Hi. I'm Sya."

Ever the one to let people know she spoke Chinese, Kimmy introduced herself. In her perfect Chinese accent, she said, "My name is Kimmy Lancaster. What's yours?"

Ya-Shin and Peggy laughed.

Ya-Shin twisted her face.

"We don't speak Chinese. Yeh, it's one thing that most people assume. She looks Chinese; therefore, she speaks Chinese. We get it all the time."

Peggy delivered less attitude than Ya-Shin.

"Sorry. We don't speak Chinese. Did I hear that your name is Kimmy?"

Sya sided with Peggy.

"Well, I guess we all have one thing in common," Sya said.

"I'm Peggy."

"Ya-Shin. Peggy and I are studying public health here at JHU."

"We're both grad students. I'm studying global affairs and human security. Kimmy, my red-headed Mandarin-speaking best friend, in case you haven't noticed, is studying innovation management and technology commercialization."

Sya abruptly changed the pace of the conversation. "How old were you when your parents adopted you?"

"Three," Sya said.

"Same," Ya-Shin and Peggy said in unison.

Sya whispered to Kimmy.

"Well, this is awkward."

Ya-Shin and Peggy overheard Sya and grimaced at each other.

"It is," Peggy said.

"Yes, second that. Uncomfortable," Ya-Shin added.

Peggy became further irritated by Sya's behavior, and said: "By the way, didn't you know that all Chinese girls have good hearing, and we are always ready to discuss erroneous assumptions and conclusions about adopted Chinese girls."

Sya felt provoked.

"Well, let's see. We have black hair. We were adopted the same year. From the same orphanage. We don't speak Chinese. All at JHU. Done. Am I missing anything?"

Kimmy couldn't stand Sya's tone.

"Sya, what are you trying to accomplish here?" Kimmy said.

Ya-Shin reacted to Sya's attitude.

"Here's another one. Sya, you're an ass. We're not. This conversation is not going anywhere. Maybe we should go."

"Wait, don't you want to meet the performers?" Kimmy said.

The two girls moved next to Kimmy.

"Sure. Why not? That's what we came here for anyway."

The dragon dancers infiltrated the lobby, and the crowd reacted with excitement. The performers – Kai Jing, Wong Bao, Li Wuji, and Wu Zhao – worked the room like celebrities.

Kai Jing eyed Kimmy and approached her. He wiped the sweat off of his brow and introduced himself.

"Hey. My name is Kai Jing. This is Wong Bao, Li Wuji, and Wu Zhao. How did you guys like the performance?"

Kimmy coyly answered.

"Kimmy here. Sya. Ya-Shin. Peggy. We all go to school at JHU. The performance was great. Which dragon part were you?"

"The tail of the yellow dragon."

"Oh, you mean the ass?" Kimmy said.

Kai Jing laughed.

"Yes, well, we don't call it that. I normally play the head, but our tail dropped out at the last minute."

Wong Bao explained further.

"Fred didn't pass chemistry. Gotta keep our grades up to participate."

Kai Jing grabbed Kimmy's hands and locked eyes with her.

"You seem so familiar to me. Have we met before?"

Sya laughed aloud.

"Oh, if you've ever met Kimmy before, you wouldn't forget. Look at that hair."

Kimmy couldn't take her eyes off of Kai Jing.

"You guys wanna go get a beer? Sya lost a bet, and the first three rounds are on her."

"Wait, what bet did I lose? What are you talking about?"

"The race in the rain, my dear. So easily you forget," Kimmy said.

Wu Zhao added his two cents.

"Wouldn't pass that up."

"Well, if I'm paying, we go to Ottobar," Sya said.

"Too noisy for me," Ya-Shin added.

Kai Jing agreed with Ya-Shin.

"I'm not that into death metal."

"OK, fine. Kimmy, you suggest," Sya said.

"Red Maple on Charles."

Kai Jing gave Kimmy a high five.

"Classy joint!"

Kimmy swung her head left and right and flipped her red hair for emphasis like she always did. They all laughed.

"Great atmosphere and a good fusion menu," she added.

Kai Jing used the moment to rib Kimmy.

"Red. Red Maple, it is."

Sya turned to Ya-Shin and Peggy.

"Will you join us?"

They looked at each other.

"You OK with that?"

"Sure."

Kai Jing motioned to Kimmy.

"You ride with me."

The Red Maple

Sya, Peggy, and Ya-Shin arrived at the Red Maple and looked around for Kai Jing, Kimmy, Bao, Wuji, and Zhao. No luck. They hung around the door for a few minutes. A waiter approached the reception desk.

"Sorry. A few minutes. The receptionist is seating other guests."

"Can we get a table? Somewhere quiet. Maybe on the garden terrace? We are also waiting for another group of people."

Sya turned to Peggy and Ya-Shin.

"They can just meet us when they get here. I hate standing at the door."

The hostess escorted them to the back of the restaurant and sat them in the garden terrace.

Sya didn't waste any time.

"So, where do we start?"

Ya-Shin put her phone in her purse and without looking at Sya asked, "Are you always this uptight?"

"Just trying to get to business."

"OK. Let's get to business," Ya-Shin said mockingly.

Peggy felt annoyed by their interaction.

"And just what is that business, Sya? You're not the only adopted Chinese girl in the world, you know. There are thousands of us. If anything, we should be kind to one another."

"Jump right in, Sya. No small talk. No need dancing around what you want. OK. Do you want to talk about what it feels like to be abandoned? Or never fitting in? Do you want the medical term for what most of us experience? Reactive attachment disorder. Normally, we are charming to strangers and give hell to our families. However, it seems like you got it backward. Hell to strangers. Do you give hell to your family too?" Ya-Shin asked.

While Peggy and Ya-Shin's reaction shocked Sya, she knew that she deserved what they were dishing out, and she understood exactly what they meant. She was guilty.

Peggy tried to diffuse the intensity of the conversation and radically changed the subject.

"I like clowns," she interjected.

"Wow, that's random, but good move," Ya-Shin said.

"They have a perpetual smile painted on their face, and no one knows what they're feeling. That's how I feel all the time."

Sya got the message and loosened up.

"I like fish."

She waited for one of them to respond.

They didn't, so she continued.

"Not just for eating. Mostly fish in aquariums. Caged beauty. Gives me a peaceful feeling in a weird sort of way. Ya-Shin, what brings you joy?"

"I don't know. I'm not good at that sort of thing. Joy. Feelings. Ask me about botany, molecular genetics, how to diagram a sentence, or the effect of micronutrients on the body, and I'm there. Feelings. Nope. Never developed them. It's too dangerous to have feelings. Don't you know? Abandoned girls don't have feelings. So, now that we've got that out of the way, what's your business, Sya?"

"Are you guys looking for your parents?" Sya asked.

Before they could answer, Sya blurted out, "I have four things in my life that take up my day. School. Eating. Sleeping. And looking for my parents. And, sometimes, it's only three. I forget to eat when I think I've found a clue or a lead."

Ya-Shin and Peggy looked at each other and shook their heads yes.

"I agree with Ya-Shin. No matter where we are, whom we live with, or where we live, it's a pain we carry with us whether or not we want to acknowledge it or admit it. How are you doing it? Is there anything you know about your time at Wulan? So far, all I have learned is that the five knocks person brought me there," Peggy said.

"Me too," Ya-Shin said.

"I learned about the five knocks person about 10 years ago. I visited Wulan, and that's what the Director said to us. My intake form had five knocks written in the upper right-hand corner," Sya said.

Peggy saw the pain on Sya's face as she told her story.

"We could share our to do list with you, Sya, and help you where we can. I'm gonna go back to Hong Kong in December to try to track down information about the five knocks person. Maybe that person has some information about your, our, parents. Ya-Shin, tell her about the begging strategy."

"Well, that's what it's called. You have a to-do list. You make calls. You write emails. You beg for information. You make a YouTube video, and a Facebook page. You make a website or landing page about your search if you have the money, and you essentially beg for information. Hopefully, one day someone who knows someone who knows someone who knows your family will see the video and contact you."

"Like seven degrees of Kevin Bacon. He's my bud. I mean, like the seven degrees of separation principle," Kimmy said.

They all laughed.

"And sometimes, blind luck swings in your favor," Peggy said.

"Well thank you both you for looking past my misbehavior. I didn't mean to be harsh. I was out of line."

"Sya, we understand the struggles and inner turmoil you feel. It's not often we have the chance to talk about this with someone who truly understands our story. It's complex. We can help each other. One thing we should remember here is that meeting our birth parents doesn't guarantee that we'll be unburdened by what we feel now. The situation may become even more complicated. And, no one can prepare you for what it feels like to be rejected for the second time. Our parents may not want to see us or have anything to do with us."

"For me, the question 'who are they?' is stuck right here in my throat. It won't go away. What could be worse than this?" Sya said.

Share This Video

After the meeting with Peggy and Ya-Shin and hearing their story, Sya felt a renewed sense of purpose in her search for parents. She hadn't felt this kind of positive momentum in a very long time. Seeing those two girls and getting some insights into the things that they were feeling gave her a great deal of comfort. Their empathy and their apparent understanding of what she was feeling overwhelmed her. She knew she had to be more proactive.

On this day, she enlisted Kimmy to help her out.

"It's noon. Where are you?"

"Give me a break. Driving up your driveway now. Twelve noon on the dot."

"Good. I need your help. And where were you last night?"

"Will tell you when I get in. Bye."

Sya set up the camera for her YouTube video, and then ran downstairs when she heard the doorbell.

"Oh my God. You look. Well. Like you were up all night. What happened?"

"Nailed it. No sleep. Kai Jing and I...after we left you guys, we dropped off Bao, Wuji, and Zhao, then we went to a karaoke bar, then, then. We had breakfast at IHOP, and oh...I'm in love Sya. I spoke Chinese all night with Kai Jing, and he told me stories of when he was a kid. We drank wine. We ate waffles. Well, not at the same place, of course."

Kimmy danced around the room like a crazy person.

"Are you trying to tell me something?"

"Well, yeh."

"Spill, Kimmy.

"He wants me to..."

Kimmy jumped on the bed and outstretched her arms, then wrapped them around her shoulders, hugging herself.

"Meet him tomorrow at the University of Baltimore Diversity & Cultural Center for the Chinese circus juggling class. AHHHHH!"

"Oh, this is...uh. . .serious. Really? Juggling."

"Come on, Sya. Can't you be happy for me? You can come too. Haven't you always wanted to learn how to perfect your juggling?" Kimmy said.

"I'm there already. Let me put it on my calendar."

"Don't you remember? Your dad was trying to teach us. He always said that there's so much joy in learning how to juggle. You need some joy in your life, honey?"

Sya mocked Kimmy with a crazy arms juggling move.

"Wait, are you making fun of me? You are. You're making fun of me. Sya, I love Chinese culture."

"Right. It's juggling today, marriage tomorrow."

"And what's wrong with that? Oh, I see. You think I'm going to abandon you too. Get over it."

"Look, Kimmy. You hardly know this guy."

"I hardly know you and look how far we've gone."

"And she goes in for the kill..." Sya said.

"Sorry. What do you need me to help you with today?"

"I think they called it a begging campaign. Or something like that."

Sya showed her a two-page list.

"Peggy and Ya-Shin gave me a long list of things to do to try to find clues about my parents."

Kimmy read the list aloud.

"Register in a DNA database, explore all local hospitals near the orphanage, develop a YouTube video, develop a Facebook page, create and promote a website, prepare flyers to put around the orphanage or the nearby hospitals, interview others from the orphanage, place ads in local newspapers, use some kind of medical reason, if it exists or even make one up to lure people into responding or make them feel some compassion for your causes. What? Sya, this says to use some kind of medical reason – if it exists or even make one up – to lure people into responding. OK, that's pretty aggressive. And not honest on top of it."

"Right! You could see how this process could turn honest, ethical people into, well, liars."

She showed Kimmy her Facebook page.

"I'm almost finished. Next on the list, a YouTube video. I need your help."

"Whatever you need," Kimmy said.

"Just want to find my parents. Help me with this. I'd like to sit on this stool. It'll make me seem tall."

Kimmy stabilized the camera, while Sya tried three or four different backgrounds on the wall. The girls created lots of commotion getting the setup right.

"Too plain."

Sya tried another background.

"Too dark."

Sya positioned a sizeable Asian fan on the wall behind the stool.

"That should work. Asian, but not too Asian. I'm ready for action."

"Let me turn on the camera. Wait. Your lip gloss is feathering."

Kimmy touched the corner of Sya's mouth and wiped off the extra lip-gloss.

"Hey. Did you hear about that adopted guy that was looking for his father? He found him. It was Charles Manson. The guy was Charles Manson's son. Creepy. That's like finding Adolf Hitler is your father. Maybe you're a descendant of Genghis Khan, Universal Ruler who laid a lot of seed throughout central Asia and China."

"Genghis wouldn't be too bad. He controlled, what was it, about 12 million contiguous square miles of land. I could take on the role of being a landowner."

"Well, he sure wouldn't approve of you doing this video. He never let anyone paint his portrait, sculpt his image, or let his head go on a coin. You wonder why? He would never have let this whole nation of girls go up for sale or allow a wholesale adoption of his people. As cruel as he was on the battlefield or in the bedroom of so many women, he had the heart for women, children, and livestock. No selling or kidnapping of women. And if you stole anyone's livestock, you'd get killed. Just like that. Too bad he died from injuries sustained when falling off a horse."

"Give me a break. Why are you so hung up on Genghis Khan? Come on. Let's just get this done."

"Trying to be helpful. Useful context. Didn't go to JHU for nothing. Got all kinds of useful and random facts in this brain," Kimmy said, as she positioned herself behind the camera.

"OK, Sya. Reporting for work. Barbara WaWa ready?"

Sya nodded.

"In three, two, one."

"Hi. My name is Sya Cynee' Porter. Well, that's my adopted name. I'm Chinese. Chinese American. I'm one of over 400,000 girls adopted from China. If you haven't heard, China has a one-child policy. One child per family. They want boys. Girls get pushed aside. I was left on the steps of the Wulan Orphanage in Hong Kong by someone that we orphans have come to know as the 'five knocks' person. Whoever it is delivers babies at the doorstep and consistently knocks five times on the orphanage door. If they hear five knocks, they know they will find a baby on the door stop. I, like a lot of Chinese girls, don't have many clues to go on, so we beg for information and for anyone to help us with our search. I've always wanted to find my parents and ask them: "Why? Why did you abandon me? Why did you give up on me? How could you do this? Can you help me to understand?"

She reached away from the camera for the folder and pulled out several pages.

"This is from the orphanage where I was adopted. I wasn't supposed to find this, but, well, I guess my adoptive parents were gonna tell me eventually."

She held up the note written by Meiying.

"My mother's name was Meiying. Apparently, I was born in a Hong Kong hospital in 1987. That's about all I know."

She put the folder down.

"If any of this makes sense to you, can you email me? I'll follow any and all leads. My email is syaporter@gmail.com. Thank you for any information you can provide. Oh, please share this video."

The Blue Scarf

Twenty people, including Kai Jing, Kimmy, and Sya stood watching a juggling demonstration by skilled Chinese circus performers. Scarves, balls, and rings were flying everywhere. About 10 minutes into the presentation, the performers started throwing the items to everyone in the room to engage them in the activity. Small groups formed as they tried to keep the juggling toys up in the air. Each person in the room picked up ones that had fallen, and they threw them back into circulation as the circus performers maintained the rhythm of the juggling activity.

Some people got hit in the head by a stray ball or juggling ring. Everyone laughed at the antics of others, especially the antics of Kimmy Lancaster. In her spare time, she had mastered juggling and performed as a well as the circus performers.

Kai Jing watched with admiration.

"One more try. Here ya go. I'm going to get 30 revolutions this time."

With precision in her throws and catches, she delivered on her promise. The whole room clapped. She bowed. Kai Jing appreciated her progress.

"OK, show-off. Next time, let's run it together with five scarves."

Kimmy put her scarves in the box and turned back to Sya as she left the space.

"One minute. Restroom."

Sya followed.

"Behind you."

They each entered a stall.

"Kimmy, how is it that you always seem to fit in? Wherever we go."

"I don't know really. But, if I had to pin it on one thing, it would be, well, um...you just need to consider other people's needs and wants. Always take time to smell the roses in the garden that you're visiting."

"Kimmy. Wait a second. Are you saying I'm selfish? OK. Maybe I am. I guess it's my mask for hiding my fear. Fear that I'll lose everyone or everything in my life. You know the Wizard of Oz, right?"

"Yeh. Who doesn't?

"I kinda feel like I'm the Tin Man."

Sya summoned her best voice and sang the Tin Man's theme song.

"When a man's an empty kettle, he would be on his mettle...If I only had a heart. I'd be tender, I'd be gentle and awful sentimental, regarding love and art...or something like that. I think I skipped a few lines."

Kimmy clapped.

"Stop, I know it wasn't that good."

"Well, my dear Sya, we can work on that."

"My singing?"

Kimmy flushed the toilet and didn't answer.

"What? My heart?"

Kimmy stood up on her toilet seat, looked over Sya's stall and loudly announced, "Sya, my dear, Kimmy is here."

"Ewwww. Get out! Can you let me do my business? I sing one bad song for you, and you think you have the permission to watch me finish my business. Call me selfish, but I don't want to be giving in that way. Go wash your hands. You're crazy. Crazy girl."

"There you go. You do have feelings."

Sya walked out of her stall and rolled her eyes.

"Let's get out of here."

They washed up and headed back out to the juggling training.

Kai Jing approached Kimmy.

"Ready for some juggling, couples style?"

"I'm game."

As Kimmy walked away to get more scarves, Kai Jing handed Sya a blue scarf and whispered: "You hold this. And when I say eleven, throw it to Kimmy with the same timing as the other scarves. I'm counting on you, Sya. Don't miss a beat."

The scarf he gave her seemed heavier than usual.

Sya opened her hand slightly and noticed a stunning diamond ring tied to the end of the blue scarf she was holding. She put it away as Kimmy walked toward her.

"This time, let's get up to at least 40 revolutions with five scarves and two people," Kimmy announced.

Kai Jing started the rhythm.

"We got this. One. Two. Three. Four. Five. Six. Seven. Eight. Nine. Ten. Eleven."

Sya threw the scarf, which was weighted down by the ring tied to the end of it. Kimmy lunged to catch the scarf before it hit the ground.

"Sya, is this a trick? Are you trying to mess me up? This one is heavier. What the heck is on this scarf?"

She examined it closer.

"Wait. Wait a second. This is a...a ruh, ruh, ring?!?"

She looked up at Kai Jing, who was smiling a Cheshire cat grin. He pursed his lips, moved his mouth side to side, then put on his best growling, cowboy voice.

"Why, yes ma'am, it is."

Like a bad actor that had done the scene far too many times, he dropped down to the floor on his knees a bit too hard. He moaned.

Sya and Kimmy tried not to laugh to honor the seriousness of the situation.

Kai Jing cleared his throat. In Chinese, he asked: "Ms. Kimmy Lancaster, will you marry me? Will you be my lawfully wedded wife?"

The whole room witnessed the exchange and started clapping.

Kimmy joined Kai Jing on the floor and got on her knees to embrace him. She gave him that bouncing kiss he had come to love, saying yes each time she pulled away her head.

"Yes."

They kissed.

"Yes, yes, yes," Kimmy exclaimed.

The crowd encircled Kai Jing and Kimmy, as they stood and shared a lover's embrace. Sya slowly backed toward the door and slipped out before Kimmy noticed she was gone.

My Necklace

Sya and Kimmy arrived together at the Charleston Restaurant. "So, what's my big surprise, Sya? I can't believe that you have kept this from me for so long."

"Not yet. Be patient. We are almost there. You always do so much for me. It's my turn."

The hostess took the two of them to the restaurant's wine library. Sya had rented the entire space.

"I read about this idea in *Glamour*. The best way to plan a wedding is to rent a space like this and have all the everyone come to you. So, ta-dah..."

The hostess opened the door. Sya had put together a mini-bridal show with food vendors, DJs, photographers, bridal gown companies, caterers, shoe vendors, vacation planners, and more.

"It's all here. Under one roof."

Kimmy moved about the room like a kid in a candy store. She took two bites out of a cherry chocolate cupcake.

"I can do this, right?"

"Absolutely! Take it all in. This is for you."

"Sya, thanks for doing this for me. My mom would've..."

Kimmy's face tightened.

"OK, Kimmy. No getting all sad on me."

"Sya, will you be my maid of honor?"

"Whew. I'd love to be in your wedding! I thought you'd never ask. Of course. Just don't make me wear a lime green bridesmaid dress! It just ain't my color, if you know what I mean."

"Do I have to do all this in any particular order?"

"Nope."

Kimmy grabbed Sya's arms and pulled her toward the massive wedding gown rack.

"OMG. Wedding gowns. Sya, you've gone all out. I want to try all of them on."

"All yours. Do it in any order that makes you happy."

"Look at this. Let me try this one. Wow!"

Kimmy took a heavily beaded dress to the lady's room to try it on. She put the dress down, and then she came back out for a pair of shoes.

"Need shoes. Size 9."

She pulled a couple of pairs off of one of the vendor's table.

"Back out in a minute."

Sya thumbed through the bridesmaid dress book and handled several of the fabric swatches. She walked over to the sweets table and picked up a pink cupcake. She took a big bite of it, and looked at the ceiling as she chewed it.

Kimmy interrupted her.

"You who. Let me make this moment about me. Look at this magnificent gown. Princess I am, am I!"

"A princess times 10."

"Whaddya think, Sya? Is it me?"

"Turn around. Let me zip it up."

Sya struggled with the zipper.

"I can suck in a bit."

Kimmy drew in air.

They both laughed.

As Sya zipped up Kimmy's dress, she thought about her feelings for Kimmy and wondered whether she should use this moment to let her know how she felt about their friendship.

Sya could hardly contain her nerves. She wasn't one to communicate her feelings on a regular basis. In fact, she rarely communicated her feelings at all. At this very moment, though, she had mustered the courage.

Sya smiled as she readied herself to tell Kimmy how much she appreciated their friendship and how much she loved her like a sister.

"Here we go. Got it. Turn around. Let me look at you. Wow. This is THE one."

Sya grabbed Kimmy's hands, and they stood face-to-face, eye-to-eye. She was ready to share her feelings with Kimmy. She smiled and gazed downward.

"Uh, Kimmy. What is this?"

Sya picked up the necklace charm and examined it carefully.

"Kimmy, um, what is this? This is my necklace. Why do you have my necklace? Excuse me. But, did you take my heart necklace? What's going on here?"

Kimmy pulled the necklace away from Sya, trying not to break it.

"Give. It. To. Me. Really, Sya. Really. I do not believe my ears. How could you jump to a conclusion like this? I've been your friend for how many years now? Do you realize that you're standing here, right in front of me, surrounded by..."

She flails her arms toward the vendors.

"...by all of this, and you're accusing me of stealing. Of taking something that is not mine. I'm your friend."

"OK. So where did you get it?"

"Look here, missy. This is not your necklace. And you're going to stand there and accuse me of stealing your necklace. Wow, that says a lot about our friendship."

"My necklace is a one of a kind, from China. How could it ever end up here? On your neck. Got anything to say for yourself?" Sya asked.

Kimmy couldn't stand Sya's negative attitude and uninformed probing.

"And one more thing, missy, I don't need things as you do. And, even if I did, I wouldn't stoop so low as to take something from someone that I consider a dear friend. Apparently, you don't value this friendship in the same way."

All of the vendors stopped what they were doing and watched Sya and Kimmy argue.

"You know what, friend, I'm out of here. This is a big mistake. All this. You can just shove it up your..."

The vendors' eyes widened.

Kimmy stopped short of saying what she really wanted to say.

"No, I won't stoop that low. And for the record, this was a gift from Kai Jing's mother. Maybe you need to start looking for the truth in your own house."

She stormed into the lady's room.

Sya stood there in shock.

After a brief moment, Kimmy came back out.

She yelled at Sya.

"Unzip me. Now."

Kimmy raced into the dressing room, changed quickly, and then raced out.

The vendors, in a state of shock, stared at Sya.

"OK, already. I thought it was my necklace. You can go. Get out. Just get out. You're not needed anymore."

Letting Go

About a hundred Washington and Baltimore elite lined up at the gangway of the Yacht Raven, a custom built replica steamship docked in the Baltimore Harbor, for Kimmy and Kai Jing's wedding reception. The smell of fried crab permeated the air, and an animated Manhattan Transfer cover band played loud enough to be heard all across the harbor.

Sya and Kimmy stood at the center of the vessel admiring the intricate details of the nine-layer wedding cake. Kimmy had never seen a cake of this magnitude. The shape reminded her of a beautiful spaceship all decorated with beads and lace. If you looked at the top of the cake downwards, the bottom layer looked like a four-leaf clover with icing flowers that looked like waterfalls coming down the side of the cake.

"Kimmy, thanks for taking my call last week and giving me a chance to apologize."

"Sya, no apologies necessary. Yeah, come to think of it, maybe one was necessary. Look, I'm in this friendship for the long haul. I accept your apology."

"Through thick and thin?"

"Friends for life through thick and thin," Kimmy said.

"Kimmy, it's the one thing that's been consistent in my life. Our friendship."

"I'm glad to be there for you, Sya, and to make amends, and I made sure I got your favorite. Atwater's steaming hot crab soup. I didn't know if I could get any. There were so many other Chinese New Year celebrations throughout the city requesting Atwater's soups. You need to try this. It's heavenly dee-vine."

They both sampled the soup.

"Mmm. Atwater's will never let you down."

"Gotta have the best for the who's who in DC-Baltimore region."

"Kimmy, is that the former Ambassador to China? How did you get him here?"

"He and his wife are close friends with my mom and dad. Kinda, my surrogate parents while my real ones are out of the country. Look to your right. That's the Mayor of Baltimore and a Baltimore Orioles' pitcher. He's kinda cute. Maybe I can fix you up with him. Betcha five bucks, he's got his uniform shirt under that tuxedo."

They both laughed.

"Sya, look. Far right. In the back."

"Kimmy, who's the red-lipped lady in the black suit?"

"Don't stare. Apparently, she's a long-time friend of Kai Jing's father, the guy to the right of the beer keg."

"He seems a bit uptight. Like he was at the wedding. Almost constipated. I'd like to be a fly on the wall during one of their conversations. Where's Kai Jing's mom?"

"She's at the hotel. After the wedding ceremony, she told Kai Jing that she didn't feel well enough to attend the reception and said something about her legs having some unusual swelling. I'm worried about her. She said it was jet lag or something. But, it seemed like something more serious. I just saw her for a couple of minutes before the wedding. She's so beautiful."

"Isn't it weird meeting your mother-in-law just a day before you marry her son?"

"Na. Well, yeh, kinda. That's just how it worked out. I guess she likes me. I think she likes me. I hope she likes me. Oh, my God. I sound like a very nervous bride who doesn't know her mother-in-law. I can tell you this. She seems oddly familiar to me and reminds me of that lady we met when we visited the Hong Kong orphanage. Just an older version. She's all grey now. Anyway, Chinese women look all the same to me. I just wish my mother and father were here. I'm both sad and happy now. Kai Jing and I'll swing by Kathmandu and visit them at the Embassy before we go to Bali for our honeymoon. They said that they have another reception planned for us. Lancaster style."

Sya loved hearing about Kimmy's parents who were both polyglots who had traveled the world working at U.S. embassies.

"Oh, the life of diplomats."

"If she were here, she would have told me, 'My dearest Kimmy, you see, those Chinese lessons did pay off.' I fought her tooth and nail about those lessons when we were stationed at the Embassy in Beijing. As a four-year-old, I had no appreciation for learning another language. Truth be told, I hated, hated, hated learning Chinese. However, I picked it up to native fluency in just a year and impressed my classmates and the Chinese staff in the Embassy with my abilities. Here I was. This flaming redhead squirt with green eyes spouting perfect Chinese, well Mandarin, to be exact. I had fun being the novelty of the moment."

Sya cleared her throat.

"You always have fun being the novelty of the moment!"

"That's the truth. It was all meant to be. My mom. The visionary. Gotta love her. And, I'll have my kids speaking Chinese from the get-go."

"Kids? You? Wait, are you prego?"

"No. Just talking about kids."

Kimmy waved at Kai Jing, as she marveled at his broad smile and good looks.

"Absolutely. Kids. All in good time. There's Kai Jing. Let me get over to him. I've left him alone far too long. Sya, thanks again for doing this for me. I owe you big time. After we finish here, Kai Jing and I have a spa date. All of this wedding stuff is stressful and quite overwhelming. I need a massage before we leave for our cruise. Later gator. Enjoy yourself, OK? Mingle or something. There are a lot of good-looking, rich guys here. Can I see you have some fun? Promise me."

"You bet," Sya said as she hugged Kimmy.

Sya, still the loner, explored her surroundings. She picked up her fourth drink from the bar and roamed to the upper deck port side. She walked to the front of the boat and leaned on the railing as she scanned the harbor.

In the corner of her eye, she noticed the red-lipped lady and Chu Shang, Kai Jing's dad sitting alone on the top deck, secluded from the loud music. Though they were leaning toward each other as if telling secrets, Sya was able to overhear what they were saying. She walked toward them and stopped behind the short set of stairs leading to the captain's deck on the port side of the yacht and continued to eavesdrop.

Trying not to get noticed, she stood still so that she could overhear the details of their conversation.

The woman spoke with a slow, gravelly voice – the voice of a heavy smoker.

"This had never been done before, so there was no possible way to predict the outcomes," she said.

The woman released a quasi-evil laugh.

Sya shuddered.

"You did well, Chu Shang, and we were able to keep China under the radar."

Chu Shang stared pensively across the Baltimore harbor and replied with a tone of regret.

"Yes, the nuances of diplomacy. I'm surprised no one has figured out the connection between China's most favored nation status and the implementation of the one-child policy."

"Chu Shang, China's population explosion was controlled. Be proud of what you did."

"Proud? Yes, I feel pride. And shame. Grief. Guilt. You name it. These ugly feelings haunt me night and day, coupled with a never-ending knot in my stomach. That knot that comes with knowing that you've done a grievous act."

"My dear, Chu Shang. China required an urgent measure. You're China's hero. You're the architect of creative and meaningful social engineering. You did that."

"What I did was destroy the basic unit of the Chinese society – the family. Not sure I would tag that as meaningful."

"It was brilliant and beneficial for America," she said.

"Exactly. And disastrous for China. Government officials took it as a license to control people. To program their lives. There is widespread coercion. Economic penalties many people can't afford. Forced abortions. Partial births. Women with broken hearts. Girl babies thrown in the street gutter. Men. Many with no wives. A nation of bare branches."

"Chu Shang, you've committed no punishable crime."

"Maybe not, but I have committed a crime against humanity. I have been instrumental in disintegrating the social fabric of Chinese society."

"OK. So maybe you didn't think it through," O'Grady said.

"Our centuries-old tradition of a preference for males coupled with the one-child policy has resulted in the wholesale slaughter of girls."

"You can't change tradition. That is not your fault."

"But, I'm at fault. For this mess. But mostly, for abandoning Kai Jing's twin sister, Guli. Fate gave me a boy and a girl. Tradition and the one-child policy that I created strangled me. I allowed it to destroy my family."

Not being able to take any more of this conversation, Sya quickly ran to the lady's restroom and hid in a stall. For the rest of the afternoon, she drank and wandered through the passageways on the vessel. No one seemed to notice.

As the party came to a close, guests exited the yacht. Sya stayed behind. Standing on the top deck, dangerously leaning forward, she watched Kai Jing and Kimmy follow the crowd.

As they turned around to wave to their guests, a drunken Sya screamed so loud that she drew everyone attention.

"Kimmy. Kimmy! Did you know that Kai Jing has a sister? What? Why are you looking at me?"

Sya turned her head upward to the sky and yelled even louder.

The crowd continued to stare.

"Kai Jing has a sister. Her name is Guli," Sya screamed.

The crowd pushed Kimmy and Kai Jing further away from the boat toward their awaiting limousine.

Chu Shang, who was still on the boat, maneuvered his way through the crowd to reach Sya.

Without being too obvious, he grabbed her by the arm and pulled her aside.

"Young lady. You're drunk and know not what you speak of."

Sya pulled away.

"And who the hell are you, Mr. Man?"

"I'm Kai Jing's father. Chu Shang. You shouldn't be yelling things like that."

"Why, I don't have anything to hide? Kimmy is my best friend, and she should know if Kai Jing has a sister."

"Can we go somewhere quiet?"

Sya leaned forward.

"I like fish."

Chu Shang didn't understand.

"You want something to eat?"

Sya pointed to the building on her right.

"The aquarium. The Baltimore Aquarium."

The two of them walked past the yacht control room, and by the time they reached the gangway, everyone had left except for the boat crew.

Chu Shang escorted a drunk Sya off the boat.

Sya struggled to walk as they headed to the aquarium.

"Mr. Man. Can I call you Mr. Man?"

Sya stumbled on the dock. The water was rough, and the aggressively bobbing paddleboats caught her attention.

"Let's go on one of those. Right there."

She leaned forward to the paddleboat with the dinosaur head and nearly fell into the water.

Shang grabbed her by the shoulder.

"I think the aquarium will be safer."

Tell Me

Kimmy and Kai Jing laid face down on the massage tables. Two Filipino ladies – Rhea on Kimmy and Rosario on Kai Jing – massaged their legs. Kimmy lifted up her head and looked over at Kai Jing wondering if he felt the same way about what they had both experienced at the dock.

"We should have stayed and helped Sya. She seemed drunk."

"She'll be OK," he said, not lifting his head off of the table.

Rosario pushed harder on Kai Jing's leg as if she were working on behalf of Kimmy, who most likely expected a different answer from him.

He moaned.

"Ugh. Lighter, please!"

"Sorry, sir," Rosario responded.

Kai Jing continued to speak.

"It's good we got the cruise out of Baltimore. That saves us a lot of time and hassle. After all this, I didn't have the energy to fly to Miami."

"Well, not to change the subject or anything, but, um. Do you have...?"

"Just say it. You know we can tell each other anything, baby."

Rhea massaged Kimmy's legs more aggressively as if to help the conversation along.

"Do you have something to tell me? What did Sya mean when she said, 'Did you know you have a sister?' What was that all about?"

"Kimmy, just remember that this has nothing to do with our relationship."

"Kai Jing, not telling the whole truth about something is the same as lying."

"I love you Kimmy and will not let this or anything keep us apart. I made a promise that..."

Kimmy sat up and dismissed the two women from the room. Kimmy crossed her arms as she listened.

Kai Jing continued: I'll start from the beginning. My mother worked at the Wulan Orphanage. Oh boy. I swore not to say anything, but here goes. I often visited the orphanage just to comfort my mother. There was always a sense of melancholy surrounding her. While I was there, she would move from crib to crib propping up bottles for the Chinese babies. Nearly all girls. I'd follow her and watch as she would look longingly at each baby. Initially, I'd be hands off. I'd just hang out by her side as she would do her work. I never could understand why she continued to work at this place.

"Kai Jing, this is something you may never understand," she would say. "Little emperor."

I would often overstep my boundaries and tell her that the orphanage was a dump. She wouldn't react right away. She continued to prop up the baby bottles with her back turned to me. Then, she would quietly say, "One day it will not be. Look at these girls. They have no one."

She would take a deep breath and then turn toward me with tears in her eyes and say, "Each morning I come here, there are five or six more new babies. Girls. All girls."

"Well, you can't save the world," I told her.

When I said that, she slapped me across the face. I turned around and sat down in a chair in the corner of the room hanging my head in apology, as she continued to prop the baby bottles in the cribs. I remained silent. What more could I say? I apparently did not understand what she was thinking. All I knew was that she was here at this bleach-filled orphanage for some odd reason, and she wasn't willing to tell me what exactly was going on in her mind. Frankly, I didn't know what to do or what to say when this subject came up, and she wasn't willing to share her feelings with me. I felt like an outsider to that part of her life. It was then that she dropped a bombshell on me.

"I have arranged everything for you to attend graduate school at Johns Hopkins University in Baltimore, MD," she said.

"Arranged? Baltimore? Where the hell is that? Sounds like an offshoot, broken-down city in England," I told her.

"Near Washington, D.C. It's a good school," she said.

I questioned her with an anger that I should never have exhibited. "You have arranged. What? How? Why? And did you pick my coursework too? Oh, this is good news. Controlling my life, are we?"

"You can choose your courses when you get there," she said. "There is an important reason that I've chosen this place. When you were born, the nurse at the hospital..."

"Wait. Hospital. Are you changing the subject? What hospital? What nurse? How is this connected to a school in Baltimore?"

I was super confused by what she was saying to me. She cried, deep from her belly. Frankly, I had never seen my mother cry. Chinese women just don't do that in front of their children. She touched her belly and said: "The night that you were born, we thought there would be two girls. Your father could not allow anyone to know about this birth. Two girls. That's the fate of death in China. No one could know of this birth. Fellow government workers were fired for breaking and disobeying the one-child policy. So, we...he, he had plans to abandon both baby girls in Hong Kong. Then, we would go back to China and try for a boy. That was the plan. All done in secret. Plain and simple. In the beginning, when we were told that we were having girls, we told no one of my pregnancy. Not even family. We could not chance losing your father's government job. In the hospital, he paid a large sum of money to a nurse to..."

I asked, "To do what?" and she didn't answer me.

She said: "He let me hold both of you for some time. But, I knew it had to end. Later that evening, the nurse came into the room and took my baby. My baby girl. Guli."

Kimmy looked lovingly at Kai Jing. He was holding back tears as he told her the story.

"That's what I named her. Guli. My two girls. Xiaoli and Guli. But, I did not have two girls," she continued. "As the nurse took

Guli away, she whispered, 'Wulan.' This place. I learned later that this compassionate woman who was being paid by distraught families to destroy these girl children would take the babies to Wulan Orphanage. Families never questioned what she did with the babies. They thought she must have destroyed them. But she didn't. She always brought them to safety."

"Is that why you moved here when father retired?" I asked.

"I begged your father to move to Hong Kong. I believed that if I worked in this orphanage that one day I'd see Guli walk through the doors. Hoping against hope that she would return in search of me," she said.

I helped her to position a bottle in the crib.

"Kai Jing, I didn't know what he told that nurse to do. I could only hope for something good for my child, my daughter."

"OK. A sister. You're telling me that I have a sister. So you toil in this god-awful place hoping against hope that she would come back?" I asked.

"Perspectives change when your heart is filled with something good. Kai Jing, you must not be so selfish and cold. You will never know the power of the love in a mother's heart for her daughter, her children."

"So, Guli's alive?" I asked.

"You may not remember, but you were here when she came to Wulan. She came with her mother and this obnoxious and boisterous, but beautiful, redheaded girl named Kimmy Lancaster."

She also had fond memories of you, Kimmy.

"Oh do I remember that girl," I said. "I was mesmerized by her striking green eyes and flowing red curls. For me, it was like...like love at first sight. She played in the courtyard with me while you were meeting with the other girl and her mother. We had a meeting of the minds."

"Is that it?" she asked me.

I had to smile. She thought I might have kissed you or something. It crossed my mind.

"That other girl. Was that Guli? That was my sister?" I asked.

"She remained quiet. I knew from the silence that I had met my sister on that day."

"So, what do you want me to do?"

"Kai Jing, you've received everything you wanted in this life. Fine schools. Expensive trips. The life of a king. Spoiled. To the point where you don't even care about people. You never stop to think about others. There is more to life than this. Now, it's your turn to give back. Find Guli. I have her address in Baltimore. She's at University of Baltimore."

"How do you know all this?"

"Just do a Google search. You will soon know as much as I do. The amount of breadcrumbs people leave behind is remarkable."

"Mother, how do you know about breadcrumbs? Wait. You know about Google?"

My mother always surprised me with her ingenuity.

"Befriend her," she said. "Take care of her for me. Protect her. And Guli must never know your father or the deed he has done. I'll sacrifice my relationship with her to protect her from knowing the truth. It was by your father's hands and his one-child policy that she was abandoned."

"And father," I asked.

"Your father must never know that Guli lives. He paid a nurse to get rid of her. To destroy her. Kai Jing, you will leave for Baltimore in two weeks."

"Great," I said.

"There are more women to choose from in America. Easier to find a wife there. What is it now 108 girls to every 100 men in China? Odds certainly not in my favor here. Not exactly sure that I want a Chinese girl anyway. Too stiff. Maybe I can hook up with that Kimmy girl," I told her.

Our conversation was interrupted by another loud knock on the orphanage door. We both started counting 'one, two…' together and stood still, listening carefully for how many knocks we would hear.

As the knocks continued, we looked at each other and mouthed the numbers: Two, three, four, five. Then, we both stood up. With that fifth knock, we knew full well that there was another girl baby at the door. I looked at my mother who was crying.

"It's my turn," I told her.

Kimmy, I was so selfish. Because as she was telling me this, I thought that this would give me a chance to see you again. All things considered, I didn't fully agree with what she was asking me to do, but I thought that it could work out in my favor.

I never forgot that day we met at Wulan. I harbored a sincere wish to see you and be with you again. It may have been puppy love when I first saw you. But, that feeling never went away. I can't explain it. It was just there. This is the truth.

Kimmy sat up on the massage table.

"Sya is my best friend. You know that. Why didn't you tell me before now? I don't know if I can ever trust you."

Kimmy stormed out of the spa area.

He got up to chase her and his phone, which was in his jacket pocket, rang.

He turned around, pulled it out, and answered it.

"Yes. Yes. When? Where? Baltimore Sinai Hospital."

Kingpin of Misery

Sya and Chu Shang walked toward the aquarium entrance. Hundreds of Chinese girls and boys, though mostly girls, of all ages with their parents, stood on the sidelines of the activity celebrating the Chinese New Year.

Chu Shang zigzagged through the sea of children near a private area in the aquarium. Still drunk, Sya followed him.

"Meiying. Does the name Meiying mean anything to you?" Sya asked.

Chu Shang kept walking.

"I should not have come here," he said.

Sya curled her nose and mocked his Chinese accent.

"I should not have come here."

Chu Shang stopped, turned around and stared eye to eye with Sya.

"There is a book in every family library that's best not opened," he said.

"Oh, that's prothetic...prophetic. Are you talking about your library? Is that what you're saying?"

Sya raised her voice louder.

Mothers of the Chinese children backed away from Sya and Chu Shang.

"Oh, it's because YOU have something to hide. I get it. Listen to me. You told that woman on the boat that your son has a sister. Does Kimmy know that Kai Jing has a sister?"

Chu Shang shrugged.

"If Kimmy knew, she would have told me. We're best friends, you know."

Chu Shang leaned toward Sya as he said: "A U.S. delegation visited China twice in the early 70s."

"What are you, like, a historian or something?"

"Listen to me. Please, what is your name?"

"Why do I need to tell you my name?" Sya asked.

Chu Shang grabbed her by the shoulders.

She winced.

"During the 70s, when the U.S. delegation visited China, a high-ranking government official befriended me. We met. Here."

"Oh, this is getting good. Yea. You met a high-ranking government official at the Baltimore aquarium. Whoop ti do. Whoop whoop ti do. Go on. I should have another drink and put the seat up, I mean my feet up. Where the hell is this going?"

"No, not at the aquarium. At the Baltimore Country Club. In secret. America needed a puppet."

"OK. This is way over my head. And in this state, it's drowning me, Chu Shang. That's your real name, right?"

"It was a chess game. Over a chess game, an expensive cigar, and a couple of glasses of bourbon, we masterminded the world's greatest population experiment. The one-child fiasco."

Sya slid down the side of the wall, put her face into her hands, and cried uncontrollably.

The room cleared.

Chu Shang paced, not knowing what to do.

Sya looked up at Chu Shang.

"Then what?"

"With this deal, I watered down China's power and inflated my bank account. I didn't know if it would work. I tried it, and it did. Chu Shang. America's best-kept secret. America's best kept puppet."

"Right. A little man with so much power."

"The U.S. wanted me to put in place a two-child policy. That was the original offer. They wanted China to take part in a global two-child policy. They knew that I was in Deng Xiaoping's pocket, so I was their patsy. I came to the table with something more. I counter-offered. More for China and more for me. I would write and implement not a two-child policy, but a one-child policy, if the U.S. gave China a most favored nation status designation, and gave me $20 million. Under the table. I needed something for me. Who can live on a measly Chinese government employee's salary? The money was part of the deal. I made the money part of the deal without Deng's knowledge."

"So the one-child policy and the designation of most favored nation status are connected?"

Chu Shang shook his head yes.

"Whoa," Sya said.

"You can thank me. High stakes for China. Even higher stakes for me. I saw this negotiation as a way for my family and me to get out of my less than average state of life as a government worker."

"With a very serious lapse in judgment," Sya added.

"On one hand, I thought I was doing the right thing. From a population standpoint. The policy was good for China. I truly believed that population control could save China. Save the planet. Even brake global warming. The $20 million was..."

Sya, still feeling dizzy from the alcohol, channeled Bob Marley.

"Hey, mahn. Dontcha not lee-son to Bobbie Mar-leh. The greatness of a mahn is not in how much wealth he gets, but in his integrity and ability to affect those around him positively, mahn."

Chu Shang didn't really understand her Bob Marley reference. He motioned Sya to move to another part of the aquarium.

"I was lured by financial gain and didn't consider any consequence. For my country or my family. My grievous mistake was..."

"Sentimental doesn't work for me, asshole."

Her gait still unsteady, Sya pulled away from him and headed for the exit.

Chu Shang grabbed her by the arm.

"Let me go. You're finished as far as I'm concerned. I don't need to know anything else from you."

She pulled away again and didn't answer.

As she turned around, his phone rang.

He didn't answer.

"Kingpin of misery. THE Kingpin...what am I doing here with you?"

His phone rang again.

He answered.

At the same moment, Sya received a text message from Kimmy: "Come right now. Sinai Hospital. Room 318. Urgent."

Chu Shang's eyes widened.

"When? Surgery? Sinai Hospital."

Sya heard that Chu Shang had received a similar message.

"OK, this is getting weirder and weirder by the minute. We just got the same message. Off to the Shy Nye hospital, we go. I can drive."

"Did you say, Shy Nye?

"Yup."

"I'll drive."

"Whatever. You're still an asshole. And, Kai Jing has some 'splaining to do wif me."

She handed him the keys, and they headed out of the aquarium to the parking lot.

Call Me Guli

Sya and Chu Shang circled the parking lot three times. No space. He drove back around to the hospital doorway and motioned to Sya to get out of the car. "Get out. I'll park the car."

Sya got out, tripped on her shoe, and fell. Chu Shang got out and walked her to the front door. She struggled to get away from him, so he let her go.

Almost hitting another car trying to park, Chu Shang drove around and found a parking space at the far end of the parking lot. He got out of the car and raced through the parking lot, through the front doors of the hospital, and through the lobby to the elevator. Out of breath, he stuck his arm inside of the closing doors so that he could enter the elevator, which housed Sya and Madeline.

"Oh, God," Sya said. "Him."

They were all headed to Meiying's room.

Sya and Madeline continued their squabble.

"I didn't mean to do this to you, Sya. I only thought that I was helping and if..."

Sya refused her explanation.

"Just get out of my way," she said.

Sya pushed Madeline aside and bumped into Chu Shang as she shifted to the other side of the elevator.

Sya's phone vibrated.

"Where are you, Sya?" the text from Kimmy read.

The elevator door opened.

Sya stayed in the elevator and responded to Kimmy's text.

Chu Shang and Madeline headed toward Meiying's room.

Kimmy and Kai Jing were on Meiying's left side. She looked pale, and her eyes were half open.

Kai Jing held Meiying's hand.

"They are taking her in for emergency surgery in about 20 minutes. You made it just in time."

Meiying, with her eyes closed, whispered to Kai Jing, "Where is she? Where is my Guli?"

Sya ran into the room.

She stopped dead in her tracks.

She could hardly take in the sight.

Kai Jing, Kimmy, Chu Shang, and Madeline.

She looked at everyone in the room, one by one.

She stared at Meiying.

"I remember now. I know you. From before."

She felt dizzy from all of the alcohol.

She reached for the heart on her necklace and started to back out of the room to distance herself like she's always done.

"Could Meiying be her mother?" she thought.

The room remained silent and motionless.

Sya could feel her face tightening and her breathing change as she uttered: "You were the lady in the orphanage."

Meiying slowly spoke, with difficulty.

"I went to work at Wulan Orphanage, hoping that you would one day return."

Chu Shang walked over to Sya and Madeline and guided them to the bed. He stood guard by the door.

"Each day I was there. I went file by file. Thousands of them. Trying to find your records..."

Meiying coughed. When she took her hand away from her mouth, there was blood.

"Trying to find your file. Then, you were there. You came to Wulan."

Sya moved closer to Meiying.

"When I saw your necklace that day, I knew you were my Guli. When you left the room, I made a financial arrangement with your mother. I thought that I could protect you. Give you a good life. Keep you away from the ugly truth. That your father was the person who authored China's one-child policy."

Riddled with shame and guilt, Madeline moved toward Meiying's bed and away from Sya, who was behaving as if she were going to attack her.

"Don't blame your mother. At that time, I firmly believed you should never know what your father had done. I wanted to make sure that you had a good life, Guli. I knew that Madeline could help me make sure that you had one."

Madeline grabbed Meiying's hand, and they cried.

"With money, you can make anything happen, right? Why not for good? I had full access to Chu Shang's bank accounts. So much money. Too much money."

Chu Shang walked to the edge of Meiying's bed.

Meiying closed her eyes and breathed deeply.

She struggled to speak.

Shang took over the story.

"There was my deal with the U.S. Government. They gave me money. They spread $20 million in 10 different bank accounts in China and several banks in the eastern United States. Meiying gave Madeline full access to all of the accounts in the United States."

Meiying pointed to Madeline, then Sya. "I did this for you. For her."

She coughed again. More blood.

"Not a day went by that I didn't think of both of you. You, Madeline for raising my dear child. You, Sya and always wondering when you uttered your first word, when you got your first tooth, when you smiled your first smile. In my mind, I played it all over and over again. Wishing I could reach out and touch you. Hold your hand. Change your diaper. I wanted to be there for everything. I knew all that I was missing. Each year on your birthday I'd go somewhere to be alone just to remember the day you were born. I'd sit on a park bench. Just me and my thoughts and memories of you. The day that I held you in my arms for the first time. The day I looked into your eyes, wiping the tears off of my face, knowing that I'd never see you again. I held you in my body for nine months. My heart was beating with yours. I never knew what a broken heart felt like until the nurse walked out of the room with you. I felt like I died that day. On those days when I got home, I'd cry myself to sleep thinking about you. I love you, my daughter. I have always loved you, more than you will ever know."

Meiying turned her head toward Sya.

"What do I call you, my daughter?"

Sya didn't know how to respond.

The room was eerily quiet.

Sya finally spoke up.

"You can call me Guli. My whole life was spent searching for you. Pushing people away because I thought there would be no room for you when we finally saw each other."

Kai Jing walked toward Sya to comfort her.

"Get away from me."

Guilt-ridden, Kai Jing hung his head. He couldn't face Sya.

He mumbled, "My life, too, has been a web of lies and deception."

Kai Jing reached out to Sya.

"Please, let me explain."

Sya pushed him away as he tried to wrap his arms around her.

Kimmy intervened.

"Sya, he's your brother."

"Yeh, I already know. Check that box. I overheard Chu Shang talking to some woman on the boat about how he got rid of Kai Jing's sister. I put two and two together and figured as much."

Sya started to back away from them both, shaking her head no and crying uncontrollably.

"Were you in on all this, Kimmy?"

Meiying tried to explain and calm Sya down.

"Sya, don't blame Kai Jing. Don't blame your mother. They were my soldiers. For taking care of my baby. I knew of no other way. I forbade both of them from telling you what I had done."

The nurse walked in to get Meiying ready for exploratory lung surgery.

"When Madeline told me that Sam had died leaving her a single mom, I had yet one more reason to give you a better life."

Chu Shang interrupted and said, "To give you back the life I tried to destroy."

Sya moved closer to Meiying and leaned on her chest.

"I don't want your money or things. I want your love. Money can't buy that," Sya said.

Kai Jing leaned closer to Meiying. She embraced them both and recalled the last time that she had them in her arms.

Chu Shang walked away from the bed and back to the doorway near Madeline.

Silence filled the room.

The nurse motioned Kai Jing and Sya to move away, as she prepared to take Meiying's bed out of the room.

Chu Shang turned to Madeline.

"There stands the child I thought I destroyed. My girl. I was such a foolish man," Chu Shang said.

"Chu Shang, life without girls is not a life," Madeline responded. Chu Shang shook his head yes in agreement.

"Women give the world beauty and feeling. They are the creative force in the universe. Men are the destroyers," she added.

Both of them walked to Meiying's bedside one last time, and they all embraced.

Sya looked up at Kimmy and smiled.

"Finally."

For Sale

Sya and Madeline sat on the front steps of the Porter house admiring the manicured lawn. Several massive eighteen-wheelers pulled up. One parked directly in front of the house. The other backed up to the garage. Workers moved the boxes one by one into the open van.

Madeline pressed the remote button, and the garage door opened. The entire space was filled with boxes and furniture.

"It was good while it lasted," she said.

"A mere fantasy. A fake life orchestrated by a stranger," Sya added.

"Sya! Why would you say that? She's your mother."

"You're my mother. She gave birth to me, but you gave me a life. You raised me."

They hugged.

"Let's leave this all behind. I don't want to live in an emotional cul de sac anymore. Remember you used to say to me, "Do you want things or experiences?"

They answered together.

"Experiences!"

They stood and raced to the car.

As they drove away, the real estate agent hammered a real estate for sale sign on the front lawn. They both waved the fake hello-goodbye wave of a bored beauty queen on a parade float...flat-handed, right, left, right, left.

Once they left the house, they gave off a distinct Thelma and Louise vibe, ready to take on the world.

Starting Over

Sya and Madeline bought ice cream at the store across the street from the water taxi dock. "Plain vanilla in a cone for me. Sya, can we start over?"

Sya nodded.

"Plain anything for me."

"Sya, I'm so sorry. Can you ever forgive me?"

"I just want simple. No more spending. No more things. No more excess," Sya said.

"You know Sya, I think that you will agree with me that money can do a lot of things, but it can't buy love."

"Or relationships. I think that's what I needed all along. The ruby red slippers were on my feet all along. Love is what we have."

Madeline laughed.

"Yeah, that's about all we have."

They walked toward the park bench and sat down.

"Mama, we'll make it."

Madeline stood up and hugged Sya knocking over her ice cream. She didn't let Sya go.

"I love it when you call me that. Can you call me that again?"

"Mama. You squeezed me too hard. Mama, you knocked over my ice cream. Mama, can I have some of your ice cream? Mama. Is that enough? I love you."

They embraced again.

Madeline got up and walked towards the neighborhood where they used to live.

"Wait. What? Where are you going? We just sat down."

Madeline was not one for keeping surprises.

Sam knew that about her.

Sya was learning it to be so.

"Come here. I want to show you something," Madeline said.

They walked a couple of blocks to their old neighborhood.

A former neighbor, Chester, drove by on his bike and upon seeing Sya and Madeline rang his bike bell and waved.

"Sya! Hey, girl. Mrs. P., you guys back?"

Madeline had a surprise of her own.

"Hey, Chester. See ya around."

Puzzled, Sya looks at Madeline as they continue to walk hand-in-hand toward the old Porter townhouse.

When they reached the property, Sya and Madeline stood facing the front door.

Sya asked Madeline, "Why are we here?"

"Memories."

"I wish Daddy was here."

"Me too."

Madeline hugged Sya as they both cried. She pulled Sya even closer thinking about all that had happened to them.

Sya didn't want to let go. Her relationship with Madeline had gone full circle. She felt overwhelmed by all that happened but carried forgiveness in her heart for Madeline. Her search for her birth parents had given her so many essential life lessons.

She closed her eyes and resurrected memories of Sam and the beautiful times with him in this house. She experienced a distinct longing to reconnect with the joy that she experienced here. She remembered the sweet Sherlock conversation with her dad as they were preparing to go to Hong Kong.

She couldn't hold back her emotions.

Madeline felt her pain. She released Sya and stared at her, saying nothing.

Sya turned her head left, then right like a dog trying to understand what message she was trying to convey.

"I never sold it."

"What?" Sya asked.

"This house. While I did give up all of my access to Chu Shang's accounts, I used some of the money to do a full renovation of this property on the inside, so that we would have a nice place to live. It's the least that I could get out of this arrangement. I think you'll like it. A lot. Dad would have liked it, too."

Smiling, they walked arm-in-arm up the steps to the house where they truly belonged.

Sya had all of the answers she needed.

Afterword

Throughout my life and professional career, I have been fascinated with everything Asia. I never understood my fascination with Asia, I just knew it existed. In my early career, I worked for the United States Information Agency (State Department) as a social scientist and Asia was my "beat." During that time, as luck or fate would have it, I traveled to the Philippines to conduct a media gatekeeper study examining news operations in Filipino television and radio stations.

About four days before I was scheduled to fly back to the United States, I met the lead singer of one of the Philippines' top show bands, Music Making Company. It was love at first sight.

Yes, it really was love at first sight – that magical moment where you just know.

Seven years and a lot of letters and phone calls later, Victor Roa and I were married. Victor came from a family of nine children. My mom came from a family of 13 children. We wanted a large family. But, having a large family didn't work out as we had planned. We got pregnant twice and had two miscarriages. We called our stillborn children that we lost to heaven Liza and Victoria. It was a profoundly sad time for both of us. I don't think one can ever fully recover from losing children in this way. To carry a child and feel the life inside of you, then have that child die before you give birth brings a trauma unlike any other you can experience and colors your hope for getting pregnant again.

After the second miscarriage, Victor and I started discussing and exploring adoption. Where? Which countries? How soon would we adopt? So many questions. I put on my social scientist hat and began exploring the possibilities.

I had recently visited Peru with my work at the World Bank and loved the spirit, the work ethic, and the gentle nature of the people there. I told Victor that I'd consider adopting a child from Peru.

I was also aware of the terrible situation in China and had developed a strong empathy for the plight of girls in that country. I was bewildered by what I found and in a state of disbelief as I learned of the involuntary massive sterilization and abortion campaigns that were used to impose compliance. This social experiment, which was designed to slow China's population growth and facilitate economic growth, was based on the generally-held belief and deeply entrenched traditional ideas that females were inferior. The policy had many far-reaching effects. It cracked open the meaning of family, kin, and filial piety, in addition to creating a global misadventure for so many girls and their families.

I couldn't let this story go. The more I researched the subject, the more it stimulated my drive to tell it. In my research, I came across a journal article that began with the following sentence: "The authorship of China's one-child policy is shrouded in mystery." When I read that statement, both the creative and maternal parts of mind went into overdrive. My curiosity exploded.

Who wrote it?

Why did he write it?

What's the story behind this decision?

Was there a bigger story?

Was this one of those behind-the-scenes decisions of a few devious government officials?

What historical evidence could I find that would inform how all of this took place?

Were there other world events of significance during the policy adoption timeframe?

What was the real "why" behind the policy development and implementation?

Each question created two more.

I became a detective for facts that could inform what was initially a personal and family decision. What I discovered in this process compelled me to develop this story...one that explored the impact this policy had on real people.

This macabre question crossed my mind: For an adoptee from China, what was the worst thing that she could find out when she embarked on the journey to find her Chinese birth parents?

I connected my answer to that journal article: That her father was the mastermind and author of China's social engineering experiment. That was the germ of the idea that drove my story.

I shared this idea with a few friends and colleagues, and from their reaction, I knew that the story would have legs. It's a discovery that would shake anyone's world.

I have come to love Sya with all of my heart and soul. She represents the wonderful children who lived in spite of the one-child policy and who bring joy and happiness to their "now" parents, extended families, and friends.

In some figurative way, I have adopted my baby girl from China. Sya resides wholly in my mind, my heart, and on these pages. I was with her on the journey. I have allowed her to come to life on these pages so that she could speak for all of the girls who were not so lucky.

⌘

Since my college days, I have been an ardent and vocal proponent of women and gender issues. In 1984, I published an article on comparable worth in *Career Woman* magazine, where I focused on how the cable television industry was rapidly expanding at a pace that positioned it as a gender-blind industry where talented women were tapped for major leadership roles. This was the perfect example of the "non-discriminatory forces of supply and demand." On average, the industry emerged with a more significant proportion of women leaders at the helm of cable television operations.

William French Smith, then U.S. Attorney General, provided the opposing, but somewhat complementary viewpoint for the article. While he didn't agree with me on the comparable worth issue, in principle, he did support the idea that comparable worth was not a task for a federal bureaucracy, which neither had the time or the human resources to implement such a policy. When governments overstep their boundaries, the results are often deleterious.

We must all appreciate and uphold the value of girls and women across all strata of society, including business and government.

We should work to create equalities in the workplace.

We need to remove gender bias and unnecessary barriers that create gender gaps.

We need to speak out.

We need to speak up.

We need to eliminate the conditions that prevent any human being from reaching her or his intended potential and excelling in the various spheres of the human experience. This is our obligation.

It is an honor to be an agent of positive change that challenges convention. Many more of us need to take on this role.

About the Author

Donna has authored numerous articles and three books including the globally distributed *The Value of Water: A Compendium of Essays by Smart CEOs; The Ultimate To Do List When Your Loved One Dies: Before & After the Funeral;* and *Propaganda, Public Diplomacy, and Idea Invasion: The Story of USIA's Worldnet.*

As Chief of Party for the Securing Water for Food Technical Assistance Facility, a multi-lateral government-funded, incubator-accelerator and recent finalist winner of *Fast Company's* World Changing Ideas Award, she catalyzes social impact entrepreneurship in the water-ag nexus with innovators who are addressing the world's super problem – how water is being used for agriculture.

Donna has worked previously as a management and branding consultant for international organizations and is globally recognized as a champion for water, sustainability, agriculture, and the environment. An internationally accredited business communicator (ABC) and certified development project manager (CDPM®), she was one of 10 social scientists to conduct research in a world capital for the U.S. Treasury's first redesign of the $100 bill. She traveled to Almaty, Kazakstan and conducted focus groups on money practices with citizens from all socio-economic strata.

Donna holds a Ph.D. in international communication, has worked and traveled in 43 countries, and sings lead in Harbor City Music Company, an internationally-ranked (6th place – 2018 Sweet Adelines International Competition) barbershop harmony show chorus. A direct descendant of the 11th governor of Louisiana, Donna is also of Cajun heritage.

To communicate directly with the author, send an email to donnavincentroa@gmail.com, or write on twitter.com/ donnavincentroa and linkedin.com/ in/ donnavincentroa. Post a photo of you reading the book! Thanks!

THANKS IN ADVANCE FOR READING MY BOOK.
PLEASE TAKE A MOMENT TO PROVIDE A REVIEW ON MY "FIVE KNOCKS" AMAZON.COM, BARNES & NOBLE, AND GOODREAD BOOK PAGES. I APPRECIATE YOUR COMMENTS AND FEEDBACK.

SINCERELY,
DONNA

Notes

71586743R00128

Made in the USA
Middletown, DE
26 April 2018